Lostart Street

Vinnie Hansen

For June Kono, master teacher extraordinaire, who with grace, dignity and professionalism prepared me for a career in education.

ALSO BY VINNIE HANSEN:

THE CAROL SABALA MYSTERY SERIES:

Murder, Honey

One Tough Cookie

Rotten Dates

Squeezed & Juiced

Death with Dessert

Art, Wine & Bullets

Black Beans & Venom

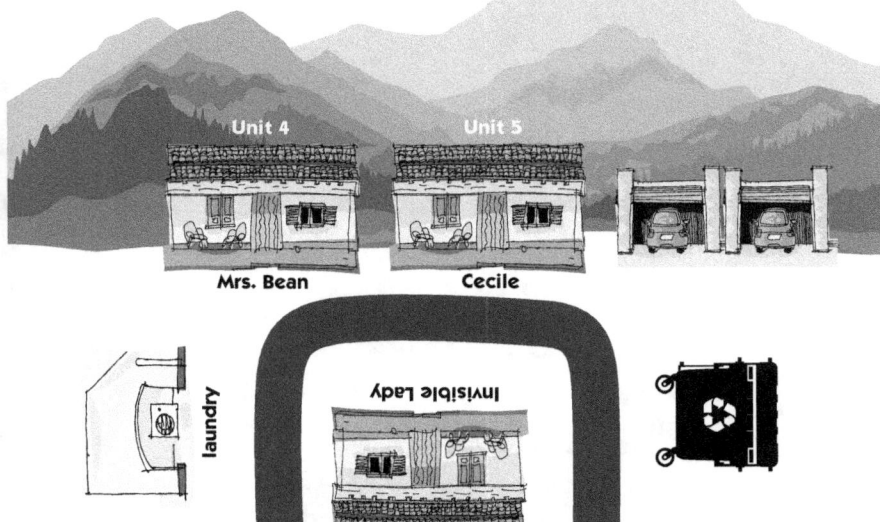

Unit 4 — Mrs. Bean
Unit 5 — Cecile

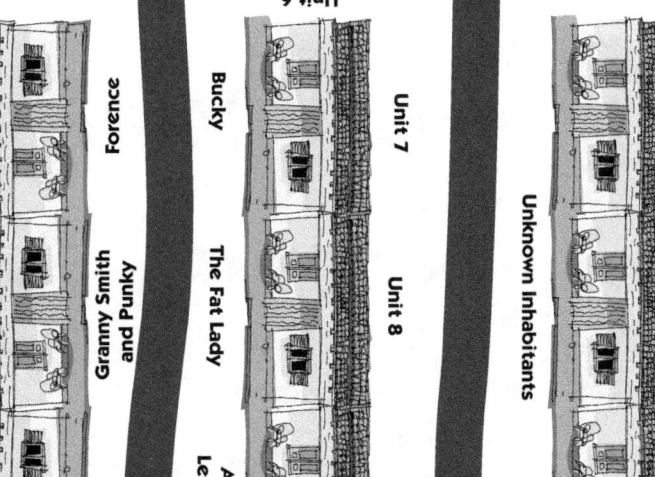

laundry

Invisible Lady
Unit 6

Unit 3 — Forence
Unit 2 — Granny Smith and Punky
Unit 1 — Vince

Bucky
The Fat Lady
Alice & Lefty Hunt

Unit 7
Unit 8
Unit 9

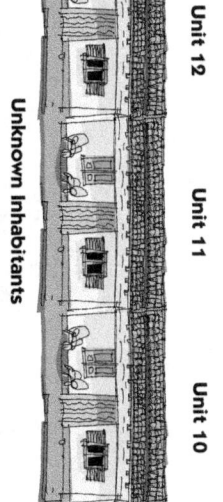

Unknown Inhabitants

Unit 12
Unit 11
Unit 10

– –Lostart Street– –

1982

The Barracks

Not a soul stirred except the two of us. The mustard-colored apartment units could have been empty.

"It's quiet," I murmured.

"Yes, very quiet." The manager, Bobbi Headland, was a tiny woman with tinted red hair and spiky eyelashes. Humans are already anatomical wonders, slender stalks balancing twenty-pound heads. Bobbi Headland added to this miracle with twiggy legs and large, Barbie-doll breasts. As we walked up the asphalt drive, all logic argued she should tip over, which perhaps accounted for her charged up, nervous air.

The alluring quiet of the place contrasted sharply with my life of MUNI buses rumbling past the flat I rented with my friend Imogene. Behind the three rows of apartments, birds fluttered in the ice plant covering a hill. A song sparrow on the tip of a stunted juniper threw open his beak and shattered the silent heat.

A humongous cat on the step of unit four, next to the vacant one, lazily lifted its head to acknowledge us.

"Hi ya, Buddha Belly," Bobbi Headland chirped. "That's Mrs. Bean's cat and folks here call it Buddha Belly. Not in front of Mrs. Bean, of course. She's very sensitive about her cat."

The vacant apartment and Mrs. Bean's stood alone, like

individual houses. A nice feature.

Bobbi threw open the door. I weighed the plusses and minuses of the place: clean with new carpet and knotty pine in a minuscule kitchen. The rent was unreasonable, but affordable given my new salary. And with my first day as a high-school teacher looming in two days, I had no time to shop. I still faced the move from San Francisco.

As I peeked about, Bobbi scrutinized the place as though trying to fathom what a single, twenty-eight-year-old would want in such a dead place. Why not choose hip downtown Santa Cruz instead of this little village? She chattered away, giving me the history of the apartments and telling me about the woman who lived across the asphalt drive in unit six. "She doesn't come out much in the day. You might not ever see her."

I should have paid more attention to this information, but it winged by.

Bobbi ducked into what I'd already decided was *my* bathroom. She stayed for a long time, but emerged seeming calmer. I should have paid more attention to that, too.

Moving in, the Sunday before my new job started, I saw the first sign of human life, two boys playing catch on one of the two driveways.

"Come on, man. Throw it right here." The chubby boy farthest from my back unit was about thirteen. He squatted and pounded the glove held to his crotch. "Aim at my nuts!"

After several trips from my Volkswagen bug to the apartment and back, I realized the "boy" nearer my unit was a mentally retarded man. He threw the ball fairly well, but the teen bobbled it.

"Jethuth Crith, you're thuppothed to catch it," the older guy said.

"You were supposed to throw it at my balls, not at my chest."

The boy waddled after the ball rolling down the drive toward Lostart Street. "You know where my balls are, Bucky?"

He scooped the baseball into his gloved hand, turned toward Bucky, grabbed his crotch and shook the handful at him.

A high, wild throw arced toward Bucky and I said a prayer for my Volkswagen's windows. The ball crashed against the roof of a prim tan Dodge Dart parked in the carport next to mine. Buddha Belly rose from his pose on the porch next door as the screen door violently opened and Mrs. Bean limped onto her steps.

Her right leg bent inward, as if it had been hit from the side by a truck. Vicious eczema riddled the thin skin of her arms, face and hands. Apparently she had once been buxom because now, the supportive muscle gone and the sustaining fat dissolved, her breasts hung at her waist beneath a floral-print, polyester blouse. Dark, wrap-around sunglasses obscured the top half of her face.

"This is a private driveway," she yelled at the boys, "not a public park. You break a window with that ball and I'll call the police."

"If I break a window, I'll pay for it," the boy said.

In spite of his snotty tone and pubescent fascination with body parts, I thought his comment showed some maturity.

"You break a window around here and you'll go to Juvenile Hall. They'll put you in jail all right. I have an uncle on the Po-lice Force."

Mrs. Bean looked too old to have an uncle anywhere. In spite of her sharp tongue, her decrepit body inspired pathos rather than fear.

Bucky and the boy trudged toward the street, muttering about "Old String Bean."

I soon discovered Mrs. Bean would gimp faithfully past my window every day to start and rev up her Dodge Dart. She didn't seem to notice me even when I was standing on my landing, but one day as I bent over, wiping aphids from my new pansies in a redwood bucket, my butt stuck in her unwavering path, her cane struck my foot, her fragile body tumbled against mine, and she regained her balance by clutching my buttocks.

"Oh, my new neighbor," she exclaimed, sounding delighted. "What is your name?"

"Cecile Knutsen."

"What kind of name is that?"

"It's a pain in the butt name. People don't put the final e on Cecile, or they call me Cecilia, or they pronounce it Sa-*seal* instead of *See*-sill."

"Would you like to have coffee with me?"

Although sure I would not, I couldn't find any ready excuse to decline the invitation.

She apologized for her poor eyesight, giving the whole history of her cataracts, the reason for her odd sunglasses. She introduced me to Buddha Belly whom she called "Buttons." Grasping her step railing, she stooped to scratch behind the cat's ears. It lethargically opened its eyes in acknowledgment and then they drooped shut again. "He's a Hima*lay*an," she said, opening her screen, "although some people say Hi*ma*layan. Now, which do you think is right?"

The question tickled my English teacher love for words, unsuspecting as I was that Mrs. Bean's story of her cat would be replayed many times, with no variation of detail, with seldom a slip of word, and always, no matter how many times I had answered it, with the same question, as if the story were taped in her brain.

On this first innocent visit, though, as she shakily poured boiling water into the instant coffee, and I restrained my anxiety that she would miss the mugs, the Hima*lay*an vs. Hi*ma*layan question sucked me in. I held forth on how people pronounce Berlin, a New Hampshire town, as they would the Berlin in Germany, while natives of the state pronounced it "BARlin."

With her hand rocking, Mrs. Bean served me the coffee, not spilling a drop. Under the small table between her two chairs, a rectangle had been cut in the floor as though someone had thought about installing a floor furnace, but then changed his mind. It seemed like spiders or worse might climb up through the opening, but I didn't say anything.

Mrs. Bean lowered herself into the other plush chair, releasing its odor of stale confinement, and continued her cat story as if I hadn't uttered a word.

"He's pedigreed," she announced. "Worth about two hundred dollars."

The cat had been given up by its owners. Actually, the people had liked the cat, but they were moving to France and did not want to see the animal suffer the long quarantine, shots, and trauma. Thus, "Buttons" had come to Mrs. Bean many years ago.

On the second cup of coffee, she told me about the burglary. Her story started by her showing me a carved black walnut box that had belonged to her grandmother. In the box had been a set of diamond jewelry: a ring, necklace and earrings.

"I keep all my jewelry in there, so I knew right away when they were gone."

"Did you call the police?"

"Of course." She slurped her coffee. "But there was no sign of forced entry. They told me it would be impossible to lift prints from the box."

"Did the thief take anything else?"

She shook her head. "You sound like the po-lice." She pushed up her cataract glasses with her middle finger, which was a little disconcerting.

I wondered if the diamonds could be Mrs. Bean's imagination, a memory given away long ago to a niece. If they actually existed, the theft sounded like an inside job, the work of a "friend" or relative. I chewed my lip. If neither of these were the case, and there'd been a random burglar, the isolation and quiet of my new apartment might not be so great after all.

An Old Story

On the night before my first day of teaching, I tried to go to bed—a sleeping bag on the bedroom floor—at nine o'clock. I wanted to be up at five thirty to dress my best in my new skirt and jacket, before I drove the twenty-minute commute. I planned to be at work by seven, giving me an hour to find out what and where I'd be teaching, before the meetings started at eight. Teachers were supposed to have the afternoon free to prepare before the students arrived on Tuesday. But I didn't count on it. If I'd learned anything during my training, it was that faculty meetings ran forever.

At ten thirty I gave up on sleeping and wormed out of my cocoon. I meandered to the kitchen and heated up a saucepan of warm milk. I poured in a bit of vanilla, one of the staples I'd brought with me from The City.

Sipping scalded milk from my sole mug, I sat at my little typing table. I peered out the curtainless window at the quiet drive, illuminated by the streetlight over the dumpster. Bobbi had told me these apartments had been motel units, salvaged from the Santa Cruz flood of 1955, and relocated to this remote plot. They were subsidized for rental to the elderly and handicapped, but a recent bureaucratic change made it possible for the owner to rent to others. I was the second integrator after Vince in unit one. "About your age." Bobbi had pointed out, arching a sandy brow.

I wedged the mug next to my IBM Selectric and ran my hand over the top of the gray typewriter. This gift from Angelo, one of the nicest things I owned, testified to my vision of myself as a writer. A deep sorrow welled up inside of me. Now I'd be using it to create lesson plans.

I'd left my file cabinet in San Francisco, but hadn't been able to abandon my stories there. From the box under the table, I extracted a cathartic piece.

Stain

I dream I have a re-live machine. It looks like Angelo's garage door opener, a little black box with a blue button and a red button. Pressing the red activator button and then the blue rewind button, I slip back in time, ready to rectify my life. I live a little, screw up, and hit the buttons again. Each time I press the buttons sooner, until finally I am nothing but a flash, like a sparkler twirled in the dark.

Outside my bare window, the streetlight developed a fuzzy halo. A tear dripped down my cheek. Not for the sadness of the botched operation, the bleeding that lasted for months, but for the end of my life as a writer and for the new life I would begin the next morning at five thirty.

Gossip

My job consumed every moment from waking until bed-time. The school had assigned me to teach four different courses in three different classrooms. The mental shift from class to class and the physical move from room to room required all my concentration and caffeine-fueled energy.

My first class, General English I, met in Annette's class-room. The room looked like a Scholastic Magazine had exploded, plastering the walls with colorful posters about books. I loved the room except there wasn't an inch of space for anything particular to my class.

On day one, Annette squeaked across the linoleum in her sneakers and pushed her record book to the side of the lectern, clearing a foot-wide space. "You can set up here." Annette was about my height, five foot six, but she had a square jaw and a build that suggested she could pick up an unruly student and use him for a caber toss.

"Thanks." My shaky hands sought my tight little bun of hair, meant to make me look less young. I secured bobby pins that had worked loose.

The frown lines deepened between Annette's eyes. Retrieving her coffee mug and a stack of papers, she settled her jean-clad butt at the teacher's desk.

After I greeted students at the door and got them seated, I pointed to my name written in cursive on the chalkboard. "I'm

Ms. Knutsen. Just remember the Kn makes the K sound, *Kuh*, then it's *newt* like a salamander, and then *sen*. *Kuh-newt-sen*."

A kid with a fresh haircut and a body like a small tank blurted, "So what is the Ms. part? Does that mean you're married or what?"

"What's your name?" I asked.

"Ruben."

"Ruben, Ms. means that my marital status is not your concern." I bit my lip. Glanced at Annette.

I could have been married now, living an entirely different life, if I'd insisted upon having the baby. But Angelo didn't want a baby, and I didn't want him to marry me because I was knocked up. I wanted to be married to a man who loved me, who couldn't live without me. That turned out not to be Angelo. He was expected to marry a Greek girl, and with a name like Knutsen, I was anything but.

I turned abruptly and grabbed my directions for an ice-breaking activity. Handing out the papers, I passed Annette's desk.

"Psssst."

I leaned down.

"Skip the salamander," she whispered. "You're confusing them."

The second day, I administered a reading test and learned that my general English classes contained students below fourth-grade reading level all the way to students who read off the top of the test's scale—post high school. In only two days I saw a multitude of reasons why the high scorers were in the low track—arriving at school without even a pencil—only bad attitudes, weak past performances, and boredom. But they weren't as worrisome as the kids whose reading had never made it to chapter books. How did I break down high school material for them?

In my freshman class I used the test scores to create groups for cooperative work, not a topic that had come up in my interview. Since I was inexperienced, the two administrators had concentrated their questions on Assertive Discipline.

After I read the names for each cooperative group, a skinny girl named Rosaura piped up, "Ms. Knutsen, how'd you make these groups? One smart person, two normal ones and one dumb?"

I already liked this girl with her snapping black eyes and spunk. Arms folded over a faded sweatshirt, she waited for my response.

Ruben, assigned to her group, said to Rosaura, "If that's the way, which one are you? The dumb one?"

Rosaura leaned over to punch his shoulder, which made him giggle.

"Stop," I commanded, but Rosaura lunged out of her seat and Ruben tipped away from her until his whole desk threatened to fall sideways.

Rosaura satisfied herself with one more slug to his shoulder. Ruben laughed harder.

I was relieved to have escaped her question and thankful Rosaura had not pointed out the obvious—that Ruben was the "dumb" one. He was a repeater, a student who was supposed to be a sophomore, but had failed most of his classes the previous year.

The view of the part in Annette's short salt-and-pepper hair had turned into a view of her face. I blushed that she'd witnessed my lack of classroom control. She rolled her eyes. She didn't believe in "group work" to begin with.

As I whizzed by her desk on the way to my next classroom, she whispered up to me, "Remember, Kiddo, don't smile 'til Christmas."

That night I first spotted Alice, from unit nine, and her dog, Dudu, during their evening circuit around the apartments—Alice, big and booming and cheerful, and Dudu, small and quiet and cute. The dog sniffed and marked the uprights in his kingdom. With shaggy hair and a lolling pink tongue, Dudu seemed appropriate for a two-year-old's birthday card, which made me think Alice might be childish. I resolved not to have a pet; the choice was too revealing.

On weekend days, Alice and Dudu's path didn't waver, so I assumed they paraded the same route when I was gone, too. Every evening they stopped across from my apartment to talk through the window to The Invisible Lady. Alice's head tipped back as all of our apartments were a step up from the asphalt.

"How you doin' in there?" Alice sang.

There was an inaudible reply.

"Well, hang in there. You know we love you." Alice would blow a kiss through the window.

Alice and Dudu were very popular with a steady stream of visitors to their apartment. I felt envious.

One day toward the end of my first two weeks, a blue van followed my Volkswagen down Lostart Street and stopped by Alice's. Naturally snoopy, I watched from my carport to see who was visiting. Eight big, burly guys, tough-looking like some of Alice's usual visitors, spilled from the van. They put on blue slinky jackets with POLICE stenciled across the chests and I thought it must be some kind of joke or something for television. Then they pulled out their guns and unloaded a German shepherd and camera equipment. About an hour later, they emerged, carrying stuff, but without Alice. No crowd gathered until they departed. I didn't feel enough a part of the community to join in. Instead, I went to the laundry room in the evening to see Florence.

Florence lived cattycorner from Mrs. Bean and me. In the laundry room, Florence drank Gallo Chablis as she washed, dried, folded and ironed massive quantities of laundry.

"Well, this place sure ain't dull," she said, slapping shut her *Psychology Today* and bringing the laundry-room lounger into a more conversational position. "People think this is some old fogey place. Looks like nothing happens here. If they only knew." She chuckled. Wrinkles etched her desiccated face. She pushed back her hair, dyed a brassy blonde.

I blushed. Florence had just delivered my original

assessment of the place.

"You mean you don't know the news, love?" Florence asked, reading my face.

The gossip, you mean. I set my wicker basket of laundry on the table.

Florence leaned forward, eagerly rubbing her hands together.

The idea she purposely dirtied clothing to arrange this kind of encounter crossed my mind. Her load in the washer was almost done, which was good. I didn't want to stay up too late, waiting for my turn, just for a fill of gossip.

"Alice in nine was busted," she said.

"Busted?"

"Um hummm." Florence sipped wine from her jelly jar and relished the moment.

I was a perfect fish, despising gossip because I was so easily taken in by the living fiction, the impromptu drama. I was a captive audience, a sucker reborn every minute.

"Well, actually, they didn't get her, just the drugs."

"Holy shit."

Florence smiled smugly, pleased to have elicited this response, and lifted herself from the ratty brown armchair, sloshing wine on her hand. She licked the Gallo from her fingers without abandoning the glass as she checked another load of clothes in the dryer. One-handed, she spilled garments into a plastic basket and scraped it across the floor to her throne.

"Not the quiet place you thought, is it, love?" Florence folded rainbows of lingerie, frilly bikini underwear, skimpy bras, and transparent nighties. With one dry, strong hand she deftly smoothed and crimped. "Interesting she left that dog with Bucky this morning, like she knew. I'd say she's long gone."

Behind me the washer thumped through its spin cycle until the whole machine rocked toward a tortuous climax.

"The stuff in her apartment would convict a saint. Granny

Smith in two died this morning, too. It's been quite a day."

"I can't believe it."

"That's because you didn't know them, love."

Gossip wasn't fiction, after all. Fiction made actions credible; gossip made them incredible. Fiction revealed, gossip concealed.

"Could Alice have been the one who stole Mrs. Bean's jewelry?"

Florence shook her head sadly, the way I wanted to do when I heard some of my students' responses. "Not Alice."

As much as Florence liked to gossip, she didn't elaborate.

The washer wound to a stop. Florence pulled flattened, mangled clothes from the machine and pitched them into the dryer. She packed the unlikely undergarments into her basket and tucked it under her free arm. "You ought to stop by some time, love."

The sad and sagging and slightly snookered woman sashayed from the laundry room. *Alice busted for possession.* I recalled the tough characters I'd seen coming and going from her apartment. *Dealing?* I never would have guessed by looking at her. However, I wasn't really paying attention. I was overwhelmed with work.

The next morning, I arrived at school an hour and a half early as usual, barely enough time to write my agendas on three different blackboards and to sort through the stuff in my school mailbox. Among other things, the mound included: the bulletin, notes from the board's meeting, a memo notifying teachers of a change in the attendance-taking procedure we'd spent an hour reviewing during the first faculty meeting, a note from a counselor alerting me that one of my students was in foster care, a notice to post in one's room regarding a start-up meeting for Students Against Drunk Driving. And a reminder that I had volleyball supervision.

Once the police were done with Alice's unit, number nine,

a man rented it, and a woman with a baby moved into unit two, Granny Smith's vacated place, across from nine. These "younger people" caused quite a commotion, especially the guy in nine. The common belief had been that an older couple was moving into nine since the manager Bobbi Headland had been seen twice on the premises with them. Apparently the manager did come around, just never when I was home.

Mrs. Bean positively declared that Bobbi had told her an older couple was taking the unit.

"Perhaps the guy is their son," The Fat Lady in eight replied. She was five-foot-nine and two hundred and eighty pounds of love medicine, in her opinion. Her license plate frames said: TRY FAT AND YOU'LL NEVER GO BACK. She filled every cell of her body and then some and delivered her opinions with force.

She planted dimply arms akimbo over her purple, hibiscus-covered dress. "I really don't give a flying fig who the guy is, as long as he doesn't play loud music. I have to sleep during the day."

Whoever he was, he passed for normal long enough for the curiosity to die.

Vince

I've always been a perverse person. Mrs. Bean, Florence of the laundry room, and The Fat Lady's suggestions that I should get to know Vince in unit one, that I might like him, primed me not to like him.

I resented the implication that I was lonely, even though I didn't have a friend within eighty miles and was the youngest person in the English Department by many years. Annette, who'd been forced to share her room with me, dubbed me Kiddo. That was the friendliest overture I'd received.

For the most part, the twenty-two teachers in the department remained courteously aloof, probably waiting to see if the new girl hired-from-out-of-town fell on her face. Two younger female English teachers with children worked part-time and disappeared at lunch. The five full-time women in the department were all single. My career choice did not seem like a match for having a relationship.

That hardly mattered. After wasting years with Angelo, I didn't feel kindly disposed toward guys. I'd fled my hometown to pursue my dream, and Angelo's immigrant story captivated me as much as his Mediterranean handsomeness. He co-owned a Greek restaurant, impressive for someone our age. If he could come to America as a teenager and reach his dream, I could reach mine.

During graduate school I'd worked at his restaurant, getting paid under the table, supporting my desire to become a writer. I didn't mind being poor. I'd been poor all my life. I was one of those idealistic sorts who didn't believe in materialism.

Then the little slip of the diaphragm.

Angelo suggested abortion. Politically I supported abortion, but it was not a thing I'd ever considered for myself. I realized then that no woman wants an abortion. Just like nobody wants heart surgery.

In between morning sickness and trying to hold my life together, I cried. Then I went to the hospital.

Afterward, my heart felt as heavy and toxic as lead. I considered myself a coward. At the same time a bitter resolve grew. Like Scarlett at the end of *Gone with the Wind,* I declared I'd never again let finances contribute to my moral choices. I would have money, a career. I would be independent, self-sufficient, a real adult, able to support a child. I wouldn't need a man.

I went back to college for another year and emerged clutching a California Single Subject Teaching Credential for English.

To a determined, "Never again," I slammed my manuscripts into the tomb of a file cabinet.

So the day I met Vince was a predictable disaster.

On a gloriously warm and sunny weekend, I decided to explore my new neighborhood. I knew only the locations of a gas station near the freeway entrance and of a shopping center with a grocery store just beyond the freeway entrance.

As I walked down the asphalt drive, a lean, athletic man emerged from unit one. I had the weird feeling that he'd been watching me and had planned this encounter. I lowered my eyes and blushed because standing on the steps above me, he was undeniably handsome and obviously checking me out.

Under his gaze, all my imperfections bubbled to the surface. After the prolonged months of bleeding and then the stress of student teaching, I was thin to the point of bony, and my cowlick-prone brown hair fell to my shoulders in a boring page cut. My confidence was about as strong as peanut shells on a barroom floor. Anger percolated up from feeling vulnerable.

"Hello." He wore only long surfer shorts and running shoes without socks. Dirt covered well-muscled legs and a light film of perspiration glowed on his golden chest.

"Hi," I said crisply.

"My name's Vince."

"Cecile," I murmured.

"See sill," he practiced. "Pretty name."

I stared at his yard. The front units had overgrown grass sloping down to Lostart Street with tangles of wild flowers near the houses. Vince had dug up the flowers and the shovel leaned against the rail of his steps.

"What are you going to plant?" I asked.

"Cacti."

"*Cacti*?" I repeated, stunned. What kind of person would plant cacti? What kind of person, besides an English teacher, would think of the correct plural?

"Yeah, cacti." He reevaluated me from head to toe. "I'm making an outdoor paradise for my lizards."

"*Lizards*." At a better time in my life I would have politely asked what type of lizards he owned, and where he kept them, but now I just wanted to flee.

He came down the two steps, but passed by me and picked up his shovel. As he stomped his blade into the earth, I lamely flapped my hand in farewell. "Bye."

I didn't hear an answer.

Point of View

Vince Meets Punky or Punky Meets Vince

It was not love at first sight. Vince thought his new neighbor would be interesting if less flesh pudged above the waistband of her cutoffs—if one could squeeze that fat up to where it belonged, although she had ample there already. He leaned lethargically against the prickly stucco exterior of his apartment and further rated his new neighbor.

She'd introduced herself as Punky Hayes and the conversation had gone down hill from there. He guessed her to be twenty-five, a really short five-one or so, and chubby, about one-hundred-twenty pounds. Plus, she had a kid. In the October sunshine, he ogled her anyway.

He inspected her exposed navel and the cleavage revealed by a bright pink and yellow polka-dotted suntop because he knew women's lib was for shit. Experience had taught him that women did not like wimpy men. They liked boldness. Forthrightness. They liked manly men.

Some of them were even attracted to jerks. The bigger the jerk, the better. Furthermore, women could say all they wanted about how it wasn't the size of the ship, but the motion of the ocean, they were more willing to sail on a yacht than a yawl. Not that he was Johnny Holmes, nor would he want to be, but he knew women noticed his goods, even uptight ones like that teacher Cecile. And, to extend his metaphor, Vince had a constant interest in sailing.

This Punky Hayes was a leftover hippie, he concluded.

His nonchalance needled Punky. She tossed back her lavish dark ringlets and squinted at him. His sun-bleached hair glinted as though strewn with mica, but he was skinny and didn't have much chest, so where did he get off looking at her like that? In twenty years he'd be picking the scabs off his skin-cancer lesions.

An insensitive jock, she summarized.

Still, he lived next door, and Punky needed to meet some people in her new home and the choices didn't seem so great. She thought of the old shrew in the back who'd make a great Halloween witch.

"Where do you work?" she asked Vince, her eyes making a full evaluation and snagging for a moment at his crotch. It looked like he had an erection.

Glancing toward the cacti he'd planted in his front yard, Vince kept an eye on Mendacity, his alligator lizard, and Hardcore, his blue-tailed skink. They twitched and slithered through the fake desert.

"Airesearch," he said, aware of her eyes and her thoughts, just as she sensed every move of her child, playing behind her on the other side of the drive. It irritated him that all women assumed they could have aroused him.

Punky savored the word "airesearch." It seemed mystical, as if related to a search of the cosmos.

"Aerospace." He spit the word like a blow dart, aimed perfectly at her imagination.

"Oh, God," she groaned, "you commute to San Jose?" She made the trip over the Santa Cruz Mountains sound like a descent into hell.

Her black hair spilled to her waist and she flashed a cavernous mouthful of slightly crooked teeth. Everything about her seemed as if it were a little too much for someone five-foot-one.

Locking up at her tease, he rifled his brain for an excuse to leave, but heat and inertia conspired against him.

"Where do you work?" he asked.

"Nowhere, at the moment." She sighed, but he seemed totally unreceptive. He was inspecting the ground and tweaking his shorts. Punky's insides settled to her feet. What if the whole fucking town proved this sterile?

"I got fired," she volunteered.

Hardcore skittered over Vince's bare toes, across the strap of his Tatamis and around his ankle. He kept his eyes on the ground to keep track of his lizards, but also because a lost job embarrassed him. He would have been less embarrassed if she'd shared she lost her virginity. "That's a strange time to move, isn't it?"

"Not really," she shrugged. "They're kind of connected. I wanted to get out of the San Francisco and I'd just begged a transfer. Then my supervisor caught me eating Oreos in the back room and fired me. He was pissed that I'd gotten the transfer and was laying in wait."

"You were fired for eating cookies?"

"Store cookies. I didn't pay for them."

The lilt in her voice suggested a trace of Gaelic that seemed out of sync with her smoky appearance. *Irish mixed with something?*

"I didn't even think of paying for them. I mean, God, they were open. Nobody ever pays for them. That's only the surface reason, of course. My supervisor liked pushing up against women in the back room, and I guess since I was leaving, he thought he could get away with it, and since I was leaving, I thought I could tell him to go fuck himself." She shrugged, again.

"You have a union, don't you?" he asked.

"Oh, yes. Retail Clerks. It's pretty strong."

"You can fight for your job."

As much as Vince hated passivity, he would have accepted a lame excuse like *But I've already moved.* Instead she said: "I don't know. Bad luck runs in threes."

Prickles ran up his spine. He jerked up from the wall as if caught on the fishhook of her illogic. "Christ, the reason things happen that way is because people like you think they do. You make it a self-fulfilling prophecy."

"What do you mean, *people like me?*"

"Boy, you're really sensitive, aren't you?"

His voice sounded both appreciative and deprecating, as though sensitivity were a fantastic trick, but one for which he had no use.

"Yeah, a real character flaw," she said sarcastically. "I better check on Todd."

Vince reached down and scooped up his alligator lizard. "Women are strange," he said. "No offense, Mendacity." He stroked her belly until the alligator lizard went still, its legs stiffly extended as though rigor mortis had set in.

Across from Punky's place, in front of unit nine, a circle of geraniums broke the tedium of the asphalt. Todd squatted there, once captivated by pill bugs, but now looking up at the man who was offering him Gummy Bears.

Todd was old enough to know he liked candy, but too young to comprehend warnings about taking it from strangers. Yet he wavered with an intuitive uncertainty.

Punky turned from her conversation with Vince and frowned to see the man bent toward Todd. The man's blond hair hung to his shoulders and framed the strange, purplish cast of his face.

"Hello," she said curtly, crossing to her child.

The man's lips melted into a stupid smile, and she suddenly regretted her suspicion, guessing he must be dimwitted like Bucky. Punky didn't want to be hard-hearted like the old lady in the back. She'd heard someone refer to her as Old String Bean. It fit.

"Gummy Bears for your baby," the man said, looking down at his brown, scuffed shoes.

As the man handed the plastic packet to Punky, Todd's caution disappeared.

"Gummy Bears, Gummy Bears!" Todd performed a two-year-old's squat-and-hop dance.

The man slipped up the steps to unit nine and disappeared before Punky could thank him.

The Budding Romance in the Barracks

I don't know what I expected of Vince, a virile, single man on the prowl, but I felt disappointed when gossip started about a "budding romance" between him and Punky, the woman with the toddler who'd moved into unit two.

I heard the "news" when Florence stopped by the open window of The Invisible Lady's apartment. During these Indian summer months, I read essays from school on the oversized landing outside my door.

Given my spot, I was destined to overhear one side of this conversation.

People called through The Invisible Lady's window as though she were deaf, although she apparently answered in a normal or even soft voice since I could never hear her. Anyway, I learned that unit one and unit two were "involved" because Florence shouted the information through my neighbor's window.

I comforted myself in a classical fashion. Vince had turned his yard into a desert habitat, tearing out the wild mint and unruly nasturtiums and replacing them with cacti and sand. Anyone who'd landscape his yard this way, covering with sand the soil that could nurture iris, anemone and ranunculi bulbs, anyone who'd do this was not the man for me.

My "sour grapes" over Angelo had dried into bitter raisins, hard little pellets that stuck in my throat. No man had touched me since I'd terminated my pregnancy, since before my credentialing and student teaching, a whirlwind of activity that left me too exhausted to care. During my training, one supervising teacher had handed me the course curriculum and said, "I've never taught this class before either. Good luck." Fortunately, my other supervising teacher had been a consummate instructor, not only of her classroom students, but also of me. Unfortunately, I'd done my student teaching with her class of advanced sophomores. At Watsonville High School, I'd been assigned classes only in the low English track.

However, two weeks into the school year, a disgruntled music teacher who'd been assigned to teach English suddenly quit, and my schedule changed to three courses in two class-rooms—much better, but nonetheless, an abrupt about-face. I now had a schedule of three American Literature classes for college-prep juniors, one section of World Literature for college-prep seniors, and to round things out, I retained the one section of General English that I taught in Annette's room. Work engulfed me. My isolation didn't even register.

I didn't feel rancor toward Punky, the new tenant in unit two. I barely knew her. After she moved in, she had been toting empty boxes to the dumpster, her child in tow, when Mrs. Bean came out on her steps to yell at Bucky.

Bucky had charge of Dudu, who insisted on the regularity of his walks, urinating every day at the same places: at the bottom of the rail on Mrs. Bean's steps, under The Invisible Lady's window on the water-meter pipes, and on the front leg of the garbage bin. Bucky had even continued the tradition of clipping ribbons on Dudu's forehead.

As far as I knew, Mrs. Bean had not minded Dudu when accompanied by Alice. But now that Bucky had custody of the leash, Mrs. Bean had developed a paranoia that Dudu would run amok and harm Buttons (Buddha Belly). This was an inexplicable theory as Buddha Belly didn't even raise his head when Dudu came to pee, and the little white dog didn't take much interest in

Buddha Belly, whose placid body hulked as large as the dog's.

On the day that Punky lugged boxes to the garbage, her boy toddling behind her, Bucky stopped with Dudu under The Invisible Lady's window.

"Hi, there," Bucky called in the window. "Juth me and Dudu taking a leak."

"This is private property!" Mrs. Bean shrieked at Bucky and Dudu. However, Punky and the child clearly thought the yell was aimed at them. They circled wide from Mrs. Bean's steps, the toddler whimpering.

"I pay to live here," Mrs. Bean continued. "I don't want that kind of garbage around here."

Punky glanced guiltily at her boxes. The child let go of the one he'd been given to drag along. Tiny and pathetic, with a child now clutching her leg, the woman stirred my empathy and my jealousy. Unmarried women with children reproached me. They'd taken the risk; they had overcome the fear of poverty, pain, and problems. Of course, she could be divorced, with alimony and child support.

As Punky collected the box the boy had abandoned and hurried by our apartments, I bit my lip and let her believe Mrs. Bean spit venom at her.

"He ithn't hurting anything," Bucky protested.

Mrs. Bean clutched the rail to keep from tipping over and falling on top of her cat, but she shook a finger of her free hand at Bucky. "That dog should've been arrested with its owner."

Oblivious to Mrs. Bean, Dudu hauled on his leash to continue his jaunt about the neighborhood. In the meantime, Punky and her child had gone down the other asphalt drive and circled on Lostart Street to return to their apartment.

Life on Lostart

Slowly I realized I might not see the manager Bobbi Headland again. If I called in the evening, she never seemed to be home. Mrs. Bean didn't like Bobbi because she came on the first to collect rent with no sympathy for those like Mrs. Bean who sometimes didn't receive their social security checks until later. Mrs. Bean called her a "heated-up divorcee."

Since I worked, I paid my rent by mail and Bobbi didn't stop at my place. Maybe she even avoided it, knowing that I needed something. She seemed the type who would evade responsibility. The judgment tasted like a penny in my mouth. I was no one to talk about shirking responsibility.

I wanted to contact Bobbi because my apartment came with roaches. And, the stove leaked gas so I kept my windows open even though most of them had no screens. Drowsy, late summer flies and desperate mosquitoes, sensing the end of their lifespans, buzzed about my home.

Worse than that, Mrs. Bean's story about being robbed had planted the idea someone might crawl through my window. And I did seem to be missing one item—a purple cashmere sweater Angelo had given me. That was the only thing, but then, after all my years in poverty, I didn't have many nice things to steal. I thought back, trying to remember when I'd last seen the sweater, whether I was sure I'd packed it.

I couldn't quite believe someone had sneaked into my house to steal a sweater, especially during a heat wave. But I wouldn't have left it to get musty in the basement of the Victorian where my friend Imogene still rented the flat.

I wanted locking screens for my windows.

In spite of these problems, I liked living on Lostart Street. It comforted me to think that probably no one could find the one-block street without directions. Students wishing to egg my apartment would have to locate my address somehow, arrange transportation to this small town twelve miles from the high school, and search for the barely paved road. Even if they found the address, they'd have to figure out that I lived in the back. I felt oddly insulated and protected by the old people around me, especially Mrs. Bean with her eye on the neighborhood and her caustic tongue.

Although my colleague Annette assured me I was doing well "for a first-year teacher," my third-period American Literature and Composition class, with thirty-seven students jammed into a small room, bristled with a barely restrained urge to baptize me in blood. I had nothing to do with the music-cum-English teacher quitting, but Annette said, "Kiddo, they resent you. They signed up for a kickback teacher and instead got you. It's a shock to their system."

Whatever the reason for their hostility, I was glad that when I left work, I also left town.

Lostart Street ran parallel to and one block from a quaint main street. After four years in San Francisco, I loved Lostart Street with its lack of sidewalks, and its many trees: wispy eucalyptus on the hill behind the apartments, a persimmon in the parking lot across the street, lemon and peach trees in yards along our side of the block, and maples thinking about fall. Mockingbirds warbled and tweeted through their enormous repertoires and finches flitted and twittered.

A small river flowed through the downtown. Fresh air

wafted from the ocean, a couple miles away. A nearby freeway entrance made my ride to work easy. As the mornings grew darker, I'd crest the hill before Watsonville as the sun was rising over blue-black mountain silhouettes. The Pajaro Valley spread and opened before me.

On the steering wheel, my fingers tapped, searching for the keys to type *crown of mauve sunrise*, hoping the words would survive the day before me.

Florence

As my new job settled down, I discovered my lonesomeness. Annette would have welcomed me at her table if I'd chosen to eat with my colleagues in the English Department lounge, but the dim room roiled with cigarette smoke.

The department chair was an ancient man who puffed cigars. And once, after spending the night at a home where the owner smoked cigars, I'd awakened unable to open my eyes. So here at the high school I chose to sit alone on a campus bench to eat my cup of yogurt and apple.

Leave it to Rosaura to ask me, in the middle of class, "Ms. Knutsen, are you a loner?"

To a freshman, *loner* ranked with dweeb. Weirdo. A *loner* was a leper with no friends. I didn't point out that I often spotted her walking alone across campus. Instead, with a crisp snick-snack, I straightened papers against my twelve-inch space on the lectern. "I'm just allergic to cigar smoke."

Since all the students knew more smoke rolled from the English Department Lounge than from the students' bathrooms, they accepted my response at face value.

"But you're not married, are you?" she asked.

I shook my head. "Let's get back on task." As difficult as this class was, I enjoyed them more than my college-prep classes. Since they'd been with me from the first day of school, they didn't bear teacher-swap hostility. Or maybe their own challenges just made them more compassionate with mine.

At home, my students' papers sometimes lasted through the weekend, but my sanity and eyes required breaks. During these intervals, I washed the dishes, laundered the clothes, and scrubbed the porcelain. I changed the sheets on the single bed I'd purchased at a garage sale down the street. Time remained.

Once I bought a phone and had service installed, I called my best friend Imogene. She was buoyant about a new guy. From then on, I couldn't reach her. She fell into love and disappeared.

I first went to Florence's apartment when the days were still warm, but cooled fast. During a restless break, I'd decided to make baklava to warm my apartment in the evening (I still had to keep the windows open) and provide a treat for my colleagues on Monday.

Angelo's mother had taught me to make the dessert. That was back when I believed I could transform myself into something Greek enough, when I was busy accumulating phrases like *kalimera*, good day. She'd been friendly to me, confident (I saw with brilliant twenty-twenty hindsight) that I would never be more than a girlfriend.

After I had purchased the phyllo dough, ground the nuts and taken out the butter to make the baklava, I realized a butter brush was not included in my collection of eight or so kitchen utensils. Once I unwrapped the phyllo, it would dry and break in seconds. I'd need a brush to spread the butter.

This state of affairs propelled me to Florence's door.

She answered with a cigarette in her hand. "Hello, love. Come in, come in." She motioned for me to enter as she padded across her apartment to turn down the radio. "I just have this on to keep me company. The T.V.'s broken."

Florence had an ex-husband somewhere, a rich ex-husband I'd heard, but she didn't seem to have any alimony. Maybe she had some social security. She made extra money as a washer-woman. She took in people's clothes and washed, pressed, mended and altered, mostly in the laundry room. In return for her domination of the laundry room, she kept the machines running and clean. She wiped the counters and table to a shine and, in spite of the constant leak from the washer, the room smelled pleasantly of detergent and starch.

So, I was not prepared for Florence's apartment. Cat hair billowed from the carpet that looked like the indoor-outdoor kind, thin, ugly, and selected by a person interested in durability, not aesthetics. Probably a good thing, since the roof leaked and an occasional whiff suggested some cat was not house broken. Brown water stains liberally marked the ceiling and peeling paint hung in great curls. The apartment had no bedroom. On the couch rumpled covers suggested the shape of the body they embraced at night. Across the room squatted the large, broken console television. A big gray tomcat rested in the back window with one eye open, as though he'd pounce out at the slightest provocation.

Florence served me wine from an uncorked jug and brushed a calico cat from one of the two rattan chairs near the door. "This baby likes any place that's toasty. She'll snatch your seat as soon as you're up."

I believed in the wisdom of neither a borrower nor a lender be and felt embarrassed to come a-borrowing, especially now that I had seen the state of Florence's apartment. I didn't want wine, but out of awkwardness, I accepted the water glass as I asked about a butter brush.

"It's nice of you to come by, love."

"What's the matter with your T.V.?" I asked to make conversation.

"Something electrical."

"Expensive?"

"Well, about eighty dollars. I was going to fix it this month, but someone stole my cigar box of money."

I told her about my sweater.

"It's someone from the neighborhood," she said.

"Who?"

She shrugged. "I thought maybe the kid who plays with

Bucky. Or maybe one of the new folks I don't know yet."

"Did you call the police?"

"Oh no. What could they do? I didn't exactly record the serial numbers. They'd blame me for keeping money in the house and having my window open."

I chewed my lip. My own windows were open, but I might be asphyxiated if I closed them. She must be right about a kid. Who else would work a neighborhood with such slim pickings?

One of the watermarks ran down toward the television. "Maybe the electrical problem is in the wall."

"A man looked at the T.V. and said it was the set," Florence stated, staring at the maple cabinetry.

These older televisions reminded me of Cadillacs—big and plush, but who would want anything so weighty?

As the wine dissolved my bashfulness, my eyes wandered up to the ceiling. "Your roof really leaks, huh?"

"Yeah."

"Does Bobbi know?"

"Yeah, but I don't make a big deal of it. I don't want her poking around. I didn't even tell her about the stolen money."

"Why?"

"Well, love," she said a bit sharply, looking me right in the eye, "so far, all the neighbors have been nice about my use of the laundry room, but if somebody complained, or if Bobbi got a bug up her butt, I'd be ousted from the laundry room and I couldn't live if I had to *pay* to wash all those clothes."

"Oh," I said dumbly.

"Besides, you know damn well that if something is fixed, the rent is raised to pay for it, and, love, I can't afford that either."

I wondered if the hole in Mrs. Bean's floor went unfixed for similar reasons.

Florence rose abruptly to get the butter brush. I'd blundered, committed some *faux pas* on my first foray into my new social life.

She jabbed the brush at me. "Besides, Bobbi Headland is a twit."

The Great Mouse Catcher

Vince was late. He stalked through the lobby of the aire-search building to the tiled corridor that led to the steps to the basement. This morning he'd been unable to find his new watch. He didn't wear it weekends when he played volleyball, but he was positive he'd left it on the stand by his bed. In the dim downstairs warehouse, Jose Martinez clapped him on the back.

"Aey, the great mouse catcher ez here," Jose announced, his "ch" pronounced like an "sh." "Aey, aey, aey."

"Again," Vince grumbled.

The other workers wouldn't bother to trap mice. If it weren't for him, they would simply sprinkle poison all over the place or would use those glue pads where the mice stuck until they died of fright or starvation or perhaps lived, in terror, waiting to be bashed. He could empathize with the mice because of his recurring nightmare. It had plagued him again last night. He had been in a race, running, running, running, but unable to move, stuck in place as if on a treadmill.

"Aey, you're the best mouse catcher," Jose said through the haze of Vince's thoughts.

"You guys need the practice," Vince yelled over his shoulder as he strode along the rows of shelves and pallets full of air-plane parts. The warehouse smelled of grease-marked pine. As he approached a small office at the end of the basement, bluish florescence and the odor of burned coffee invaded the cool dimness. From the office Vince snatched an empty gallon coffee can and its yellow plastic lid from the top of an army-green filing cabinet. The place reeked of stale cigarettes.

"The great safari hunter has arrived," someone shouted as Vince entered the dim aisle.

"Vince the Invincible," another jeered from a passage.

"It's too bad you guys don't have the balls to do it," Vince said at large to the warehouse.

A tall man named Jamal appeared like a shadow from behind him. "Damn, man. Is that what you use? I wanna see that."

The supervisor—a short, bald man—trooped down the dingy steps toward Vince. It was a rarity to see him out of his office, and Vince was surprised all over again at how spindly he was. The supervisor dressed impeccably in three-piece suits and sat in the back office from seven until three writing orders and apparently living on coffee and cigarettes. The color and texture of his face reminded Vince of potato sprouts, something that thrived and grew in a cellar.

"Glad to see you're doing your job, Vince," the Mr. Pasty Face supervisor said. Half his mouth twitched. Even fresh in the morning, he stank of cigarettes with an overlay of after-shave.

Fuck you very much stuck in Vince's throat like a fish bone. "Where are they nesting?"

Behind him Jamal guffawed at Vince's seriousness.

"The boys can show you." Mr. Pasty Face peered through Vince as though the office beyond and his scribbled stack of ash-burnt orders beckoned him. But, for a moment, he clutched Vince's shoulder. "What, exactly, do you plan to do with all these mice, Vince?"

"I'll give them to people for pets."

Jamal howled.

"Prejudice against mice is like prejudice against blacks," Vince said. "It's cultural brainwashing."

Mr. Pasty Face slid around Vince and the big man.

Jamal squinted at him. "You comparin' me to a mouse?" He sauntered off, tossing a "shee-it" over his shoulder.

If Vince had his druthers, he would leave the mice as they were, in the nests of dust balls, paper shreds and weeds in the bottom of a huge crate. The box was a perfect house for them with an open knothole and tunnels through loosely packed airplane parts.

As Vince lifted the heavy parts from the crate, the mice squeaked and scuttled toward the now taped-over knothole. He must be like an angry God to them. They had no way to know he was different than other people. Not that he was the type who opposed hunting or killing. He regarded vegetarians as mostly a bunch of hypocrites who'd squish a bug or chop a snake without a thought. Killing belonged in the natural scheme of things. Killing didn't bother Vince; senseless, wasteful acts did.

One by one he cornered the mice and caught them with a gloved hand. Contrary to the cliché, mice were not always timid. He hoisted each into the coffee can with wary respect.

More of Melancholy Monday

Like the suddenly cold, overcast sky, The Monday Blues surrounded Punky Hayes, too. She had to face the Unemployment Office. She could no longer convince herself that she was busy settling into the apartment.

Furthermore, she hadn't had the money to leave Todd with anyone—she didn't even know anyone—and Todd waddled, babbled and climbed like a monkey, with energy like his father's. The lack of alone-time was driving her bonkers.

Pain erupted in the nook of Punky's heart reserved for the baby's father. He had been a flash of lightning. He danced with abandon and fucked with abandon and they'd made this baby under a cypress tree, with crickets serenading, the scent of dewy grass against her face, moonlight slivered by the branches. She'd felt this tingle and had sensed her uterus transformed to a womb, and that was life, full of accidents and crazy things. She'd never deceived herself that this man would stay.

She flopped across her bed and cried with Todd standing beside her, patting her with soft, quizzical hands. She hugged him to her. "Don't worry, angel. I wouldn't have it any other way. You're the best mistake I ever made."

She thanked God for this wiry, healthy baby with curly, brownish-blonde hair and huge blue eyes. When she stripped him at the beach, he compared quite favorably with other two-year-olds. She had birthed him at home, and, with a maternity leave from the store, had nursed him for a while. She credited these things for his self-possessed personality. He wasn't a whiny brat like some babies.

Thinking of Todd's birth and her old life caused dread to leaden her belly. Maybe she'd made a mistake, after all. She reassured herself that The City was no place for a child, that she'd been wanting to escape since before the birth, but still, the prospect of the Unemployment Office chilled her. She'd managed Todd without becoming a welfare mother, and she would continue to manage.

She wondered whether she should dress up for the occasion or look as destitute as possible. She finally opted for natural and comfortable, a pink cotton tent dress she'd worn during her pregnancy.

When she heard the knock, she composed herself. She wiped her eyes with a fingertip of pink dress bottom. The new neighbor towered before the door.

"My name's Lefty Hunt," he said. "Can I talk to you?"

She crossed her arms impatiently, but she remembered the packet of Gummy Bears and softened. "Okay."

She couldn't see any physical deformity, only a slightly purple cast to his skin and an overall weirdness that came from the way his arms dangled like long, weighty sausages from his yellow shirt, with hands cupped into loose fists along his hitched-up pants. His shirtsleeves were pressed into crisp tents, but the man's hair was long and unkempt.

"I do have to go pretty soon, though," Punky added.

"My name's not really Lefty."

"Oh." She felt uneasy. "What's your name?"

Todd hung on her leg and peeked around it.

"It's William. But nobody would ever call me that."

Punky didn't like her anxiety. She prided herself on taking people however they came. She couldn't see anything the matter with the man, and yet he seemed deformed to her. She focused on her Zen koan to calm herself: How does a rose blossom?

"Nobody in our family was ever left-handed but me."

"Same here," Punky said, "but that's normal. Only about one out of ten people are left-handed."

Todd was popping his head to the side and then ducking behind her, over and over, trying to engage William in peek-a-boo.

"We're a special breed," he said in a voice so conspiratorial it made her shiver.

"This is Todd."   She caught the boy's head to create a diversion.

"Are you married?" the man asked.

She had faced this assumption in various forms more times than she cared to think about. She pushed Todd back by the forehead, instinctively, not wanting him to hear, for the umpteenth time, the note of condemnation.

"What did you want to talk about, Lefty?"

"Divorced?" he asked, almost in pity.

Punky mustered her iciness. "It's not necessary to marry to make a baby." She started to close the door. "I've got to go."

Lefty Hunt stuck the ball of his foot against the door. "I didn't mean to offend you," he stammered. "You know people don't just discriminate against the illegitimate."

"Get out!" She hated that word *illegitimate*. It suggested Todd was less than a real baby. Not legitimate. Somehow false. Bastard was preferable.

"They'll discriminate against anything. Take me, I'm left-handed."

"Get your foot out of my doorway!"

"Once, when I was a kid, my mom bought me these colored ink pens—"

She placed a hip to the door and added some pressure. "Don't even think about telling me how to raise my kid!"

He extracted his foot, but not like he had any comprehension of what she'd said. "You don't know how hard it was," he rambled on. "Every time I wrote with them, my hand dragged across the letters and ink smeared on my cuffs and Mama would swat me—"

She slammed the door but could feel his presence looming outside the walls.

In her bedroom, Punky tied back her thick hair with a pink ribbon and jammed Todd into a sweater, wiped his nose and checked the Velcro tabs of his shoes. Todd liked the crackling rip the tabs made when he pulled them apart. When Punky returned to the living room, Lefty was still mumbling through her door about how left-handers were more likely to be bed-wetters.

Why me? She decided the third part of her bad luck had arrived.

What Mrs. Bean Had Seen

The other English teachers lavished praise on my baklava, especially Lily and Marge, two of the other full-time female teachers. Both were in their early forties; they both had short, blond curly hair and they went everywhere together, giving rise to their nickname, the Bobbsey Twins. I wondered if they were a couple, but I didn't dare ask. If they were, they remained strictly in the closet.

At the end of the day, only one piece of baklava remained, the last piece that no one dared to eat. The piece that made one an old maid. I decided to give it to Mrs. Bean since it couldn't do her any harm. I'd already given Florence a plateful with the return of her butter brush. I wondered for a moment if Mrs. Bean would be able to crunch the nuts, but for all her other ailments, it turned out Mrs. Bean had a full set of her own teeth.

I'd bought a cheap pine rocker so I had a second chair, and I served the treat to her at my apartment. The seventy-nine-year-old Mrs. Bean liked my coffee. I was standing by with hot water to dilute it, but Mrs. Bean took a big gulp.

"Ahhh." She sighed in satisfaction like a perfect commercial. "My, this is good coffee. I don't think I ever tasted coffee this good."

Mrs. Bean then and there endeared herself to me.

She told me the whole story of the apartments being old motel units moved from Santa Cruz after the 1953 flood.

On another occasion, she had told me, as Bobbi had, that the flood was in 1955, but I didn't want to question her and thereby prolong the visit. However, she didn't continue with one of her taped stories, instead she said, "I don't think that guy in apartment nine is quite right in the head. I don't know what he's doing here, anyway. Bobbi told me an older couple took that apartment."

"Maybe he's their son."

"Well, I don't know."

"What makes you wonder?"

"Well, I don't see so good on account of my cataracts, but I hear fine, and you know I spend most of my day sitting right there by that big front window and I can see all the way down the driveway to the street even if it is a bit bleary. Well, this morning that guy from nine was bothering that new girl with the baby."

"What do you mean bothering her?"

Mrs. Bean told me what she'd heard and what she thought she'd seen.

"He sounds a little strange," I said, with reservations about Mrs. Bean's reliability.

"You know, that girl should come to me for help if she has any problem like that."

This is where I heard the major story of Mrs. Bean's life. She'd been a counselor for twenty-five years until finally her "drunken lout" of a husband had done her the good favor of dying. She'd never been able to change his ways, failing at the case she'd wanted the most to help. She was convinced he'd resisted her efforts out of perversity.

The bitterness in her voice told me she couldn't forgive him, and I didn't think it tactful to bring up the current theories of co-dependency.

When her husband had died, Mrs. Bean had shifted to helping people with "real" problems. As a middle-aged woman, she'd added some psychiatry courses to her counseling degree and eventually worked in a psychiatric ward until a man attacked her with a knife that he'd managed to sneak from the cafeteria. He slashed her throat, just missing her jugular vein, before the other staff members pulled him off her.

With shaky fingers she tugged at her collar to show me the scar. "Now don't tell anyone," she whispered, leaning forward confidentially, "but to this day I'm afraid of a nigger."

I bristled and sat stunned. I didn't know anyone who would use that word, but now I had one as my next-door neighbor. Partly to avenge blacks, I told her, in a cold tone, that I thought the new girl didn't come to her for help because she was afraid of her.

"Afraid of me?" Mrs. Bean exclaimed.

I nodded. *Yes, you old shrew.*

"Well, that's loony. I'll go down there and meet her. She can't be afraid of me."

Mice Are Nice

Vince carried the can of mice under his arm to his apartment door. He resented the way the people at work treated him like a stupid, warehouse worker when he'd been promoted to planner a year ago. He had declined the promotion and kept the basement job (with lower pay) because lifting boxes kept him physically fit and because he got off early enough to go to the beach.

His new chubby neighbor, with a bag of groceries wedged over her hipbone, kid beside her, was struggling to open her door. He trotted over to help her with his free hand.

"Thanks," she said tiredly. "God, what a day."

"You too?" She didn't seem to bear him any ill will. He felt suddenly that he would like to talk to someone, so when she asked him if he would like a cup of herbal tea, he said, "Sure," although he never drank those concoctions of leaves and twigs.

"Just make yourself at home on those futons."

Vince lowered himself awkwardly, betting she was the type who sat lotus. His nose wrinkled. Clearly she burned patchouli incense. He would like the odor if it could be cut in half. Her child stood squarely in front of him with his eyes riveted on the coffee can from which issued scratchy, scurrying noises.

"How would you like a pet for your kid?" he asked when Punky brought him the mug of tea. He noted that she handed it to him with her left hand, the skin smooth and the nails rounded and shiny.

She sat half lotus a respectable distance away, clasping her own mug of stuff that smelled like the ocean during a red tide. She touched the coffee can with her toe. "What've you got in there?"

"Mice."

She swallowed her tea and coughed. The kid, attracted by the mysterious sounds, squatted by the can.

"They make nice pets."

"I bet they do." Her nostrils flared and her nose quivered, as though the energy behind her smile needed more places to come out.

Vince pulled a glove from his pocket, put it on, peeled back the lid punctured with air holes, and inserted his hand. The mice scrambled. He caught one by the tail and dangled the scudding prize.

Todd squealed, reached forward with cupped hands and then pulled back, and then reached forward again with his index finger as if to touch the mouse where it now shivered in Vince's hand.

"Where did you get those?" she asked. "How many do you have in there?"

"About a dozen," he said. "I caught them at work."

She leaned toward him, forehead creased, and untied the pink ribbon in her hair. Thick waves slid around her shoulders and hid her face as she peeked into the can. "Aren't they crowded?"

A warm fragrance floated from her hair. "Not much more than we are in these buildings when you consider their size," Vince said.

He hated himself for sounding glib. His statement hadn't been accurate, but he didn't know any graceful way to retract it. "When they do get too crowded, they take care of the situation."

"How's that?"

"They kill each other." He wondered if that were the kind

of statement that earned him the recrimination of "unemotional," but Punky took it in stride.

"Why don't the people at your work set traps?"

"I won't let them." Keeping a firm hold on the little creature, he stroked the mouse with a bare finger. Todd stretched his fingers and tentatively touched it.

"I wouldn't have anywhere to keep it," she murmured, breathing the steam of her tea. "Do they carry disease?"

"I have an old terrarium I used for Marilyn, my tarantula." He watched for a reaction and was disappointed. But it made him take another look at the woman resting on the flowered futon. The receptionist at work shriveled at the mere mention of a "bug," but Punky looked completely absorbed in her tea and as exhausted as he felt.

Todd tried to grasp the mouse, but Vince retracted his hand. "He's not ready for that," he told the child. When he returned the mouse to the can, the rugrat squealed with glee and pried at the lid so that Vince had to hold it in place with his palm.

"Okay. I'll try it," Punky said, "but you'll have to show me how to take care of it, and I want to be able to return him if it doesn't work out."

"How about two? To keep each other company."

"What the hell," she said, "as long as they're the same sex."

"What'll you name them?"

"How about Love and Peace?"

Vince had the diplomacy not to say anything. After all, they were going to be her pets. At least she'd had the sense not to give her kid a dippy name.

He ported the terrarium from his apartment to hers. It still had a layer of sand and peat chips in the bottom and a screened lid on the top.

As they decided on the table in front of the futons for the terrarium and outfitted it with a water dish, Punky told Vince about her trip to the Unemployment Office, hours of waiting just to get an appointment to return. Todd had gotten cranky with nothing to do and the people looked so weird, she was afraid to let him out of her sight. "I swear to God all the weirdos from San Francisco have migrated down here."

"There's a Sixties time warp here." Vince placed Love and Peace into the cage. Todd watched every move.

"Well, I don't have anything against the sixties," Punky said, but she cringed at the memory of all the long hair, beards, and dirty clothes in the Unemployment Office.

"I don't have anything against the sixties, either, except they've been over for twelve years."

As Punky wondered what Vince would think of the marijuana plant in her bedroom, someone knocked at the door.

"I hope it's not that guy in nine. He's nuts." She spun a finger around her ear. Instead of going to the door, Punky slid into the bedroom where she could glimpse her step from the window.

"Hey! Hey!" Lefty Hunt yelled at the door. "I know a guy's in there, and I'll give him 'til ten to come out."

"Oh my God." Punky returned to the living room. "This guy is bonkers."

"You hear that?" Vince laughed. "Just like in the movies. He must have a crush on you."

The thumps on the door grew louder and moved lower. "He's the devil! You hear me, the devil!" Lefty's voice climbed to a high, nervous squeak.

"You go away or I'm calling the police," Punky yelled back at him, astonishing herself with the words. She had never called the police in her life, and she certainly wouldn't call them now with a four-foot plant in her bedroom.

"He probably wants attention." Vince was serious now, but annoyingly calm. "Ignore him and he'll go away. He's probably a little slow like Bucky."

"Mentally retarded and disturbed are not the same thing."

They listened to Lefty hammering on the door and yelling that he, Lefty, had met Punky first.

"That's not even a fact, Jack," Vince muttered, but not loud enough for Lefty to hear.

"This guy, this devil," Lefty screamed, "thinks love is a four letter word."

"It is, you moron!" Vince shouted through the door.

Punky tittered, but whispered to Vince, "Didn't you just tell me to ignore him?"

The yelling didn't last long because it had aroused more people than Vince and Punky and Todd. The Fat Lady, who lived across from Punky, had apparently emerged from her apartment. "How long do you plan to do that?" she shouted at Lefty.

Lefty seemed to ponder the question and stopped hammering.

"I work six nights a week," The Fat Lady continued hotly, "and I have to sleep in the afternoon. I can't sleep with that racket."

Inside of unit two, Punky stared at Vince, and her gray eyes opened like a geode into a mysterious, sparkling interior.

"I'm glad you're here," she said.

She leaned toward him and he froze, but she only touched his arm, said thanks, and flashed a big mouthful of teeth.

"You should thank The Fat Lady." He tucked the can of mice under his arm and prepared to leave.

Before settling down to his T.V. dinner, Vince set up the mice with some cheese and water and then went by his Datsun to drop off the can. His luck with getting Punky to take two of them had persuaded him to try to peddle some at the pet store the next day. At the very least, they might take them to feed to their snakes, a natural fate for a mouse.

The Rescue

The cloudy dampness of fall crept along the window as Punky woke that Tuesday and found Todd pushing Cheerios through the screen to Love. "My little munchkin," she said, squeezing the boy. But only one mouse cowered in the cage. Peace was gone.

The mouse could have climbed up the glass and nosed off the screened lid or maybe Todd had set it free. Another possibility made her intestines knot, but she dismissed it as preposterous, paranoiac. At night she locked the door and shut the windows; she would have heard someone entering. She'd ask Vince if a mouse could nudge off a screen.

Punky put on her Mao jacket and drawstring pants and worked on combing Todd's hair and dressing him as he squirmed and tried to continue his play. No one had advised her against having Todd, but her father thought she'd turned into a loose California hippie. Her mother said nothing, but regarded Punky with compressed lips and unhappy eyes.

They both adored Todd, but she could no longer endure being around the family even for his sake. Her brothers and sisters seemed to consider her stupid for not having an abortion, secretly, of course, since none of them approved of such things. Bottom line, her family was embarrassed by her. How they could maintain these attitudes as they kissed and swung and fussed over Todd angered her so much that she didn't want them to see him.

Today she and Todd had to go to the bank. Punky dreaded The Shrinking Balance. First and last months' rent and a security deposit had taken a chunk of her savings. Maybe she'd been crazy to move, but her heart had been set on the transfer. Anyway, it was done.

Stepping out to the asphalt driveway with Todd on her hip, she had only a moment to hear blackbirds squawking in the persimmon tree across the street and to feel the sun breaking through the morning mist and to think, yes, she had done right. Then a door closed across the way.

Lefty Hunt loped toward her. "I wanna talk to you," he whimpered.

Punky turned to walk away, but the man grabbed her arm. She shrugged free and repositioned Todd on her hip.

Lefty grabbed her arm again. "You stay away from that guy."

His blue eyes seemed tuned to another reality, but otherwise he looked like an ordinary person, no worse, for sure, than the guys she'd seen in the Unemployment Office. He was no beauty contest winner, but he didn't look like a psycho either.

"Keep your hands off," she said crisply.

Lefty relaxed his grip and she lowered Todd to the driveway, but the baby clutched her leg.

Then, Lefty clenched tighter. She touched the cold, purplish fingers and peeled them from her biceps.

"We're alike," he said.

A chill ran through her. "Let go of me!" She bent a finger backward, no longer concerned with whether it hurt. Todd cried and tried to crawl up her leg.

Lefty bent as though to put his lips on her cheeks. She shook her head and snatched for her child's hand, but the sudden move twirled Todd to the blacktop.

"Mamamama," he cried, hanging on to her leg and getting jerked around as she dodged Lefty Hunt.

A vaguely familiar voice came up behind them, a female

voice that demanded a salute.

"You let that girl be. You have no right to grab her like that."

Lefty stopped. His eyes widened and blinked at the approaching figure.

Todd wailed in full force now and Punky picked him up before she turned to the old lady hobbling down the driveway like Hopalong Cassidy. The woman vigorously shook a knobby finger at Lefty, her wrap-around sunglasses bobbing. "Shame on you!"

Lefty slunk toward his apartment as Mrs. Bean wobbled up and patted Todd on the back. "It's gonna be okay, little fellow," she clucked.

"Thank you," Punky said.

"I don't know about that character," Mrs. Bean said, returning to her normal, strident tone.

"I feel bad for him," Punky said. "All he tried to do was kiss me on the cheek. He's obviously not all there. I overreacted."

"Overreacted, my foot," Mrs. Bean said. "I wouldn't let him kiss me for all the tea in China. I don't know what he's doing here anyway. Bobbi told me the apartment was taken by an older couple."

"He's their son," Punky said. That's what she'd heard in the laundry room.

"Well, he's a strange one," Mrs. Bean said. "Look, if you need any help, anyone to care for the little tyke there or anything else, come on back to number four. I was a counselor for twenty-five years and . . . ."

In the middle of the driveway, Mrs. Bean played the tape of her life for Punky.

The Continuing Saga of Vince and Punky

Late in the afternoon with sweat trickling down his fore-head from a beach run, Vince rapped at her door. He felt relaxed now. If he waited until after his shower, the giddiness might return. This woman was having a strange effect on him.

The door swung open. "Boy am I glad to see you." Punky's deeply scalloped nose and full cheeks flushed. By contrast her eyes appeared green, not the gray he remembered.

He wondered what else he had changed in his fantasies. Todd peek-a-booed at him around her wide pant leg. "You wouldn't have a cat I could borrow?" he asked. The moppet kept widening its blue saucer eyes at him. In his daydreams about Punky's breasts, he hadn't thought much about the kid, either.

"God, practically everyone in these apartments has a cat except me," she said.

"Maybe I could use Buddha Belly." Vince chuckled. Then he told her about the mice that had gotten loose in his car. She stood laughing in the doorway until tears collected in the corners of her eyes. He smiled apprehensively.

"I thought you didn't believe in killing mice."

"This is different," he said. "It's natural for cats to prey on mice."

"What a rationalization," she said. "Would you like some tea?"

He confessed to being a coffee drinker and dashed over to

his apartment for his instant coffee. His favorite barrel cactus lay uprooted and tipped on its side. The culprit could be the stupid little dog that the guy called Bucky walked around the complex. But Vince's logic told him Dudu was too wimpy. The plant had been ripped from the ground.

Inside his apartment, he scooped a few handfuls of water from the tap to quench his thirst from running. He'd looked forward to the cactus's beautiful yellow blossoms in the spring. Florence had relayed to him the thoughts of the English teacher in five—her disdain for having a yard full of cacti—and Vince couldn't wait for his yard to erupt into color. He knew that teacher type. Hostile towards men, her flesh consumed by anger, her body all angles and bones, her sexuality eaten away, and her heart poured into her work. She'd learn a thing or two about cacti come April.

In the curtained dimness, Vince's agitation mounted. Punky had seemed so happy to see him, but as devoid of sexuality as the teacher, the palpable force gone. He should have run harder at the beach. Anxiety tingled along his skin, threatening to pop out through his pores. He moved to his terrarium, unfastened Mendacity from a branch and rubbed her cold, scaly skin. He held her close to his face and her imperturbable stare calmed him. "How would you like to be free?" he whispered.

When he returned to Punky's apartment, the teapot was shrieking. She made their drinks and poured apple juice into a plastic cup for Todd. The child drank from a spout on one side of the screw-on lid. Punky tried to persuade Todd to sit with them on the futons, but he preferred to toddle, with his head tipped up to drink so that he couldn't see where he was going.

"He likes to live dangerously," Vince said.

"Yeah, he's the type who has to fall down to learn," Punky agreed. "Runs in the family. Speaking of falling down, did you see your cactus?"

"Looks like a dog got it," he said.

She sipped her tea. "I bet Lefty Hunt did it." She told him about her morning, the missing mouse and Lefty's harassment.

"If he stole your mouse, I wonder if he could have taken my watch."

"Maybe, but Mrs. Bean said someone was stealing stuff before he arrived."

"But who'd want your mouse except Lefty who lusts for you?"

Her eyes unplugged. They went gray and hard as stones.

"I didn't mean anything bad by that," he stammered.

"You don't know what you mean," she said.

He thought hard, but couldn't decipher her message. He thought he'd known what he meant, but he wasn't sure now. Her scent made him act stoned. He mumbled an apology.

She waved her smooth-as-caramel hand as though to clear the air. "That's all right. I made too big a deal of Lefty Hunt."

He wished he could redo the conversation, but even if one could mend something, it was never like new again. Cracks and sorrows accumulated until eventually a thing wasn't worth keeping.

"You know what I was thinking?" she asked buoyantly, not suspecting that he loathed rhetorical questions.

That I'm a psychic, he rejoined in his head.

Punky waited, as though she sincerely believed he might know her thoughts. The silence made him uncomfortable and perspiration trickled down his side under his T-shirt. He shouldn't have drunk coffee so late in the day. It contributed to his uneasiness.

The little boy abandoned his cup and moved to a box of toys. Punky stood and swooped down on the baby's cup, her large, loose breasts jostling. She took the cup to the sink, but returned, waiting for his response.

"What were you thinking?" he obliged. She crossed her bare ankles and folded herself into sitting, without using her hands, her hips flexible and giving.

"I was thinking about the Merrow fairies."

He blinked, surprised that a person from San Francisco would choose that word.

"Not that kind of fairy," she said, as though reading thoughts were indeed second nature.

In spite of himself, his eyebrows shot up. He shifted on the cushion. "Are you into fairy tales?"

"I'm Irish."

He didn't reply.

"The male Merrow is really ugly with green teeth, and green hair, and pig eyes," she said, trying to scrunch her face into a simulation of ugliness. Todd, sensing the tone of a story, stopped tugging toys from the box and plopped into his mother's lap. "So the female Merrow, who lives in a cottage of oyster shells at the bottom of the sea, is always searching for a young, handsome fisherman to be her lover."

Is she dropping a hint?

"If she finds a man, then she'll live with him on land." Punky stroked Todd's curly locks. "They say the storms on the Irish Coast are caused by the jealous Merrow fairy."

The lilt in her voice squelched his irritation and he wondered how she'd succeeded in telling him such a story, short as it was. His taste ran toward history, nonfiction, and detective novels.

"That story makes me sad," she said.

He practiced unusual restraint and didn't say what the story made him.

"It reminds me of Lefty Hunt," she added.

"Well, Lefty is playing his jealousy to the hilt, all right."

Now the story was over, Todd padded back to the toy box.

"I think about how everybody has called me Punky all my life, same as people called him Lefty. It has affected me."

"What's your real name?"

She shook her great mane over her shoulder and stirred up that incredible fragrance. "Margaret."

Margaret definitely seemed too stiff for her, like a queen's name, but, on the other hand, he couldn't imagine her as a Maggie, either. That seemed like a name for a maid. "What effect has your name had on you?"

"Well, it makes me punky-like, short, childish, plump— like that."

"You mean," he grinned, "if people hadn't called you Punky, you might have grown taller?"

"Yeah, that's what I mean." She unfolded a leg and play-fully nudged his shoulder with her foot to show there was no anger at his mockery. "I do feel truncated."

"More likely it's made you into a punk," he said.

"Yeah, a little of that, too."

They sat silently, sifting the conversation that had passed while Todd pulled a teddy bear, brightly colored plastic hoops and wooden blocks from the box, all the fun in emptying the box, not in the playing with the toys.

"I saw a big, gray tom hanging around behind my house," Punky said, coming back around to why Vince had knocked at her door.

"I was thinking about catching that cat," he said. "If you didn't have one, that is."

"Are you serious?"

"It has dessert every night from the garbage bin. I don't think it'll be that hard. It looks like a hell of a mouser. You wanna help?"

"What'll I do with Todd?"

Again Vince exercised incredible restraint. "He can help."

"That's all right," she said. "If we're not going until it starts to get dark, he'll be ready for bed. He's tuckered out from all the running around."

Lefty Hunt had skulked to the bottom of the sea like that ugly Merrow fairy she'd mentioned, and Punky bubbled now at the surface like the escaping female.

Vince possessed radar for such bubbles. It was unfair of

women to call him insensitive simply because he declined to confuse the effervescence of lust with the gurgles of a man sinking into the mire of love.

The Police at Punky's

Admiring the stars, Punky and Vince sat on the gravel in back of the dumpster, their feet protruding toward the empty field that ran along the last string of apartments. After the crowdedness of San Francisco, Punky could breathe in this place that afforded weed-grown lots. In the city the buildings had seemed pinched, the Victorians drawn up like corseted ladies, the bay breeze caught in their skirts and turned to chilly eddies. Here the air flowed freely, brisk with the oncoming fall. The scent of eucalyptus floated down the hill behind them. Of course, she also smelled the garbage, and the tuna Vince had thrown on top, but, at least here a person could distinguish one odor from another; they weren't churned into a damp news-paper/diesel concoction.

She felt as though they were waiting for something more momentous than a tomcat. She unfolded the doubled grocery bag, to be ready, and fished in the pocket of her Mao jacket for the joint and matches. She sparked up.

Vince fumbled for the joint with his gloved hand, secured it, inhaled, held the smoke. He coughed, and handed it back.

Punky giggled.

"I don't smoke much dope," he said. "Makes me sluggish."

"You mean relaxed?"

"I guess I don't like my thoughts melting into puddles. I have these great revelations that turn out to be trivial, but I never know, maybe I can't recall them right. Maybe they were profound."

"I can see how not knowing would bug you." She passed him the joint and he took another toke.

The garbage poofed and rustled under a sudden weight. Vince leapt up, dropping the smoke. He knocked the lid brace and slammed down the top.

"Hey!" Punky scooped up the joint, pinched out the lit end, and stuck it in her pocket.

"All right," Vince said. "We've done the easy part."

As Punky eased open the lid for him, Vince bent over the edge and groped toward the hissing and snarling. The funky stench of disturbed garbage whirled up to her. Vince teetered forward, grasped the hissing silhouette by the nape of its neck, and worked the animal into the bag Punky had prepared for him. The cat would be a good mouser, all right, Punky thought.

Just as Vince was peeling off the smelly gloves and they both tasted the thrill of victory, Florence galloped around the corner toward them. Without her cigarette and jelly glass of wine, she looked naked in the moonlight.

Punky braced herself to be yelled at for animal cruelty.

"There you are, love," Florence cried to Punky. "There are cops at your door. I told them I'd find you. I wouldn't have said anything, love, but they looked like they might go in one way or the other."

"Oh, God," Punky said. "Oh, God."

Florence laid a hand on her shoulder. "Relax, love. Have a piece of gum." She shook a stick of Spearmint from its package with expertise.

"Somebody must have reported my plant," Punky choked. "God, that's a felony. What'll I do?"

"Just chew, love," Florence said.

"I think it takes five plants for a felony charge," Vince said.

The cat had quieted and stopped struggling. Punky thrust the bag to Vince. They hurried toward her apartment.

In the light of the half moon, the two men at Punky's house turned to meet them. A tall, barrel-chested uniformed deputy stood at the door and a small man in plain clothes waited at the bottom of the steps.

Florence put an arm around Punky. "Remember you're a pretty girl, love," she whispered, "and I'll be right here if you need me."

"Good evening," the sheriff deputy said heartily, tromping down the steps. "Are you Margaret Hayes?"

"Yes, sir." Her voice quavered.

"I'm Deputy Smith and this is Julio Gutierrez from Child Protective Services."

They all stared at Julio Gutierrez, an anomaly. What did someone from Child Protective Services have to do with a dope bust?

"We hate to bother you, Mrs. Hayes," the big deputy continued, and Punky let the "Mrs." slide, wondering how they'd gotten her full name. "But, we have a child abuse report on you."

"What?" Punky yelped. "That's crazy."

"Now you have to understand," the sheriff deputy said, "that a report is not evidence or proof, but we do have to investigate, especially when a caller states a beating is in progress."

"Who . . .?" Punky stopped cold and whirled to face apartment nine. She pointed her finger. "That weirdo did it!" She turned back to the two men. "Does it look like there's any beating in progress? That asshole in nine is harassing me. He even spied on me to find out my real name. He follows me around and grabs me . . . ."

Florence put a hand on Punky's shoulder. "Calm down, love."

"We don't ask for names," Mr. Gutierrez said. "We don't know who made the report, ma'am, but we do have to ask some routine questions, even though, obviously, there's not a beating in progress . . . now."

"Do you want to see my child?" Punky shrieked. "There's not a scratch—" She halted, remembering the nasty fall on the asphalt. The nut had caused that, too. *A fall.* She could imagine how that would sound. Isn't that what they all said? She felt as if she'd pop. Because of one crazy person, these men had approached her with half-baked ideas about her character and their heads full of unoriginal plots. If they could fit her into their scripts, they would. "I do *not* beat my child," she said, each word brittle as ice.

The bulky deputy hooked his thumbs into his service belt laden with weapons to combat bad people. "There are other kinds of abuse."

"What are you implying?"

"The person who made the report said your child, a two-year-old, correct?"

"Yes."

"He said the child was regularly left alone."

"That's absurd. I was right there," Punky pointed toward the trash bin, blocked from view by the other apartments, "and my child is asleep. Can't a person step outside while her child's asleep? I didn't know there was a law against that."

"I'll vouch that she takes good care of her kid," Vince said.

"This man your husband?" Deputy Smith glanced suspiciously at Vince and then coldly at her.

"I'm a friend. We're neighbors."

"What were you doing out there?" the deputy pressed.

"We were catching a cat," Vince said as though it weren't any of their fucking business.

"*Catching a cat?*"

Vince reached into the bag and hauled out the tom by its scruff. It exploded into a scratching, spitting, and growling gray flurry that leaped toward the tan uniform. The man jumped, reaching for his gun. The cat streaked toward Lostart.

"My Tom!" Florence cried. "What were you doing with my Tom in a sack?" She backed away from Punky and stared at

Vince, as if, indeed, they might be child abusers.

Punky squeezed her eyes shut. If only she could get through this evening without the police arresting her for moral turpitude or marijuana possession she'd be lucky. She took two deep breaths and silently chanted her koan.

"If we keep talking this loudly," Vince said, pivoting from Florence's glare, "we're going to wake the kid. Would you like me to bring him out here so you can inspect him, gentlemen? I think I can do that without waking him."

Punky could have kissed him.

"It would be a good idea to see the child," Julio Gutierrez agreed, frowning around at all of them.

Vince went into her apartment and emerged with Todd in his arms.

The tousled head turned to find a comfortable spot against Vince's shoulder, but his eyes stayed closed.

Julio Gutierrez shrugged. Clearly the guy could see a beating could not have been going on even when the call was made unless she'd drugged Todd or knocked him into oblivion. But Punky's heart hammered as Julio Guiterrez approached her baby.

"Most calls contain some validity," the man said. He slid up the legs of Todd's Mickey Mouse pajamas. "How'd he get these bruises?"

"I was trying to get away from that crazy guy and Todd had my leg. He fell in the driveway."

Punky chewed her lip, tears sprouting in her eyes. In truth, she'd twirled her baby onto the hard surface and even dragged him a bit. She struggled to view the situation as Julio Gutierrez must. Hired to protect children, he no doubt viewed the "adults" of the world with suspicion, as a pretty shitty and very deceptive bunch.

"We would like to see the child's environment."

Deputy Smith, wiping at the front of his uniform as though the cat had spit on it, said gruffly, "The job's not done until the paperwork is finished." A person could find the quip in every other public restroom, but the man smiled thinly as though he'd been witty.

When they turned toward the steps, Punky started shaking uncontrollably. Vince opened the door for the men and her heart burped.

She followed them in. As soon as she entered, she noticed that Vince had shut the bedroom door behind him. *What a guy!*

Florence hung back at the doorway, looking indignant and insulted, as if unsure she wanted to be associated with catnappers.

"Florence," Punky said, "please believe there's an explanation for the cat thing."

"Oh, there's an explanation for everything," Florence said hotly. "That doesn't mean there's an excuse."

"I wanted to use him to catch some mice," Vince said quickly, but softly, since Todd's ear rested near his mouth. The little gesture of sweetness melted Punky completely.

Julio Gutierrez lifted his eyebrows and eyed the mouse in the terrarium while the deputy shifted his weight and sighed at the sight of futons.

"I knew he'd be a great mouser," Vince said out the door to Florence. "He's clearly the strongest, toughest cat around."

"You can bet your bippy on that, love."

Vince motioned toward the futons with the hand cradled around Todd's bottom. "This is your total choice of seats, gentlemen."

Florence moved away, down the steps. "I have to get my cigarettes." The tone of her voice indicated they weren't forgiven just because she didn't intend to miss the action.

As Julio Gutierrez edged around the living room, stopping to open the toy box and inspect its contents, Punky forced herself to breathe.

The Morning After

In the morning Vince forgot to sign in at work, rammed a pallet with the forklift, and spilled coffee down Jose Martinez's undershirt.

"Ah, chit, man." Jose Martinez smeared the coffee with the palm of his hand. "You need to be laid, man. You're as nervous as a stud, you know, before they let it with the woman horse."

"Mare," Vince said. He strode to the back office with Martinez at his heels. Vince picked up an empty water bottle by its neck.

"Mare, tha's it." Martinez snapped his fingers.

Mr. Pasty Face barely raised his head, indifferent to the two men and to the fate of the Alhambra bottle.

Sometimes Vince felt like knocking down Martinez because the thin, tiny man with the pencil mustache acted as though he'd fried his brain with hot sauce, when, in fact, he was sneaky. Like now, the guy'd struck the exact nerve. With cocky assurance, Martinez had guessed . . . no, not guessed, stated, exactly what was ailing Vince. It was uncanny; it reminded him of Punky's ability to pull thoughts from his brain.

Vince had been with Punky all night and images, like a surreal film, tortured his mind—first a strand of hair in candlelight, then a pliable mound of breast under his hand, next the arch of her neck under his lips, tasting like her exotic scent. Not leading anywhere. In frustration, he jetted air through his nostrils.

Then he smacked his forehead because that sounded exactly like an aroused stallion.

He forced himself to think of reality to avoid a hard-on as he walked through the basement. After the police had gone, he'd wanted to sleep with Punky, but they had sat talking on the futons. She'd lit a candle to soothe herself, and her features flickered in the soft light and the scent of her hair, that harem smell, mixed with the odor of burning wax. She nestled against him, wanting to be held after the ordeal, but unable to relax. Every time she rose to check the child, his cock rose with her.

The cheeks of her butt were larger than those of any woman he'd been with. Catching the fabric of her drawstring pants, her ass divided like an apricot. He wanted to bite the fleshy roundness down to the seed, to explore her most secret spots. But Punky feared Lefty Hunt might be watching, that he might fabricate another report, and she kept popping up, rigid with vigilance.

Vince hoped she'd call the manager about that guy this morning. Water bottle in hand, he stopped at the broken pallet.

"Whatcha doin', man?" Martinez asked.

"I'm going to construct a mouse trap in my car," Vince said.

"Oh, yeah," Martinez said as though he didn't even wonder why someone would make a mouse trap in a car.

Vince wrenched a plank from the cracked pallet.

"You'll get in big trouble, man," Martinez said, "if someone sees you doing that."

"You're someone," Vince said. "See, I'll put the bottle in my car with this plank running up to the neck, and then I'll put cheese down inside the jar and the mice will jump in after it, and they won't be able to get out because they aren't so good at climbing up glass. What do you think?"

The man laughed, making noises through his nose. "You're nuts, man."

That was a response Vince knew all too well.

Her hair uncombed and her eyes bloodshot, Punky sat on the futons and thought about the large plant of Colombian in the bedroom. A decent lid of weed could cost two hundred dollars, and she wondered why she could possess an ounce or less with little worry, but a plant, raised solely for her use—cheaper, purer, and not contributing to organized crime—constituted a felony. Maybe Vince was right and one plant didn't count.

If she uprooted the plant and draped it upside down in the closet to dry, she wondered if that would be a felony since the marijuana would not, technically, be growing. It was a shame to pick it now when in two more weeks that plant would be perfect, but she had to get rid of it before she called Bobbi Headland about Lefty Hunt. There was no telling who might show up at her place.

Fear and Trembling

Force feeding my seniors *The Love Song of J. Alfred Prufrock* for the perverse, egotistical reason that I love the poem, (appropriate for our fall weather, I told them), I trembled at the heart of it:

Do I dare
Disturb the universe?
In a minute there is time
For decisions and revisions which a minute will reverse.

The lights blinked and the floor trembled. The poem must be affecting me more deeply than I thought. By the time the first dictionary hopped from the shelf, all the students had ducked and covered.

Since I didn't dare disturb the universe, it had decided to disturb me.

Elisa Dorado called from under a counter, "Come on, Ms. Knutsen. This is for reals."

The quake itself was deadly quiet, but desk bottoms clicked against the tile, pencils rolled, and the Plexiglas panes over the fluorescent bulbs rattled in warning. Squatting under a desk, I smiled meekly at the other bodies huddled and crouched on the floor under other desks, and I had the profound, humbling, and yet, quite ordinary realization that I was more frightened and just as vulnerable as my students, and, not only that, it was glaringly apparent to them. We were all at the mercy of the earth.

When the shaking stilled, after a couple of minutes, we stiffly unfurled and the students picked up objects that had fallen and then sat down, whispering assurances to one another and joking a bit about "The End."

They seemed alert and excited as they gradually gave me their attention. Then I made a stupid mistake. I asked them to pick a segment of the poem, anything from a line to a stanza, and to respond to it in writing. The excitement dissipated; it left the classroom like air from a balloon. Disappointment settled in its place.

The students could understand that I might have been too shaken to discuss the experience, but I could have asked them to write about *it*. Instead, I was afraid they might say something about what they'd seen in my face, so I had asked them to stuff their feelings. To get back *on task*.

Although there was no power after the tremor, and I was not fit to teach, school stayed in session. I was thankful the earthquake had not happened during my third period class with my brightest, largest, and most cruel group of juniors. They would have used it as an excuse for a major disturbance or would have ridiculed my ignorance.

Our campus served as an Earthquake Emergency Center so in theory I couldn't be in a better place, even if my legs kept registering aftershocks until the final bell rang.

At home, the power was out. My favorite vase had leaped to its death on the linoleum and a red rose lay in the shards of glass. A bottle of vinegar had fallen from a shelf into the sink and the sharp smell filled the apartment. The earthquake didn't damage much because I didn't have much.

The banging of Mrs. Bean's screen door startled me, and I watched out the window as Florence made her way around the unperturbed Buddha Belly. "Are you going to be okay now?"

she asked back into the apartment.

"Yes, that's just fine," came Mrs. Bean's loud voice. "Thank you for cranking that thing up for me. I guess the knob was rusty."

"No problem. That's what neighbors are for."

Florence crossed the drive to The Invisible Lady's window. "Hello," she called. "How you doing in there?"

The usual pause.

"You have candles or a kerosene lamp for tonight?"

Another pause.

"That's good. I was helping Mrs. Bean turn up the wick on hers. Do you have a radio with batteries?"

Another pause.

"Good. Sounds like you're all set, but if you need anything, you call me. You have my number."

I wished that Florence would cross back over to my place, but she probably figured I didn't need anything. I put on a good front.

When the World is Still

I had no battery-operated radio, and when I picked up the receiver of my phone, it crackled with static, so I sat in silence with my students' papers. As it grew dark, I lit my one candle.

My cheap pine rocking chair creaked, and the papers rested on my thighs like an old woman's lap rug. Since I'd lived now in California for ten years, I'd experienced other earthquakes, but they'd either been tiny tremors or I'd slept through them or I'd been in a car and hadn't felt them. This one had moved the floor under my feet and vibrated the ceiling of the classroom.

Now, as I sat in my apartment, I glanced at the top paper in the stack. The irony of having left a dying paper mill town only to be deluged with papers struck me. Anger resurfaced for how I'd handled the earthquake at school.

The student had written neatly across the top:
And when I am formulated, sprawling on a pin
When I am pinned and wriggling on the wall,
Wriggling. Sprawling on a pin. The words evoked the image of my fetus. It had been a bit over an inch, a fraction of an ounce, a worm-like creature, but with face and features, arms, elbows, forearms, hands, thighs, knees, calves, feet, a creature the size of the top joint of my little finger, ugly cute like E.T., wriggling, helplessly, for a millisecond at the tip of the suction.

Get a grip, I told myself angrily, closing my eyes and rubbing my eyebrows. Eliot was not talking about what we did to other people, but about the way Prufrock and people in general bathe in formaldehyde and hang their own carcasses over labels.

I was skewering myself on a pin of guilt. Anti-abortionists made a big deal over the beating heart, but a corpse on a pump could have a beating heart. They didn't ever focus on the less romantic, but equally important, brain, which in my fetus would have been essentially non-existent. Could you be a human without a brain? What about the idea of brain dead?

"I don't think any woman thinks it's not alive," my friend Imogene had said. "You just do what you have to do and then try to live with it."

Below the copied passage, the student had written. "School makes me feel 'formulated.'" I couldn't read any more. I cried noiselessly, feeling unutterably miserable, like a stupid perpetrator in the crime of the century, pickling brains with codified knowledge.

I put aside the papers. The doctor's vacuum had sucked the life out of me, left me dried up, without enough juice for tears as I rocked in my solitary case in the stillness of a power-less night.

Lefty Hunt

Lefty Hunt huddled in the dark, terrified. He wondered if the trembling and darkness had happened because he'd forgotten to take his meds. But he didn't think he'd forgotten. His mother had bought a plastic dispenser for him with each day of the week labeled, and every Sunday she organized his pills. But maybe it was Wednesday and he just thought it was Tuesday.

His mother would be angry if he'd forgotten to take them. His mother's eyes looked like shattered marbles. Her smile looked like a red stick you could break. Even her yellow hair was stiff and furious.

Lefty sat in the corner with his legs drawn up. He chewed on his knee and wished it weren't dark. Then he could check the calendar and the pill dispenser again. Maybe something would tell him for sure it was Tuesday.

Lefty wished he had a flashlight.

Of course, even if the Tuesday pills were gone, somebody could have stolen them. Somebody was taking stuff like Mrs. Bean's jewelry. At Tranquility House, Carl always said people took his clothes, but Carl was crazy. Lefty hoped nobody thought he was the thief just because he was different.

It was so much easier at Tranquility House where Teresa Galera gave him his meds. That was better. Then he was sure. Then he had people to talk to. People like himself. Carl and four other guys. And Mama Galera. And Joe, her husband, who did things like paint the splotches on the ceiling after the inspector came. And put on the new toilet that rocked. Mama and Joe's kids lived there, too. Anabelle had her crib in his room. Lefty liked to hear Anabelle's soft, sweet breathing at night. It calmed him better than meds. He didn't know why that facility had to close. He wished his mother had put him in another facility. Nobody here wanted to talk to him.

He wished his mother would come even though he didn't like her to come. Always he felt like that time when she'd caught him playing with himself, like she was ashamed, sorry he was ever born, like she was glass that could crack right in half.

Curled in the corner, Lefty chewed on the wet knee of his rumpled pants and touched himself in memory of that time. He thought of Punky with her thick hair and big smile. Punky who was left-handed like he was and had a sweet-breathing child like Anabelle. He wished he could be with Punky.

It All Comes Out in the Wash

Light danced in the windows of Florence's apartment as I worked up the courage to knock. I had no reason I could state for my presence. I couldn't recall the last time I'd visited someone just to visit. It was before my job, before the credentialing program, before the pregnancy . . . . The scratchy voice of a radio announcer covered the sound of Florence's footsteps so I jumped when the door opened.

"Hello, love," she said. "Come in, come in. Let me get your plate before I forget. The baklava was delicious."

"I didn't come for that, Florence. I came to visit."

A kerosene lantern burned on the coffee table and candles wiggled their flaming bellies on top the refrigerator, the windowsills, and the television. Shadows leaped on the walls. This was not right. You didn't spring a visit on a person.

Florence crossed the room and clicked off the radio.

"Good. Good. Have a seat. I'll get some wine. I hope it's still cold."

I sat on the faded pillow that served as a cushion for one of the two rattan chairs. A tomcat meowed at me from across the room in the open window.

"It's okay, Tommy," Florence clucked. "She won't catnap you."

Handing me a glass of wine, Florence curled into the other rattan chair and told me the story of the previous night, how

Punky and Vince had captured Tom. "I probably would have killed that asshole Vince if he didn't remind me of my son," she concluded halfway through our second glass of wine. "Tom has been a nervous wreck all day; he hasn't even gone outside."

"You have a son?" I could feel my eyes brighten. A tentative stir. I'd been without a man, without interest in a man, for pushing two years.

"Had."

"Oh." I'd blundered again. Never one to press, I waited, and patiently waited, having been taught that good things come to those who wait.

"He committed suicide."

"Oh."

The cat emitted a long, tortuous cry, the kind that can come only from a big, throaty tom not used to crying. In that strange room full of wavering and shifting light, my imagination, overexposed to early American authors like Melville and Poe, conjured that cry into a desperate call from her son's unresting soul.

"It's okay, Tommy," Florence said.

But the cat yowled again, in protest. The world was not okay, and he would have himself understood.

"You see, love," Florence said, finishing her drink. "He's a nervous wreck. Of course, the earthquake didn't help any." When Florence stood to pour herself another glass of wine, her shadow lurched on the wall as if it were drunk. "But you know, that Vince is so much like my son, with that tan and that sun-bleached hair, beautiful like that, love. I couldn't give him the crap he deserved."

I stayed glued to my seat like an ineffectual blob with no idea how to comfort her, stunned that she might be as needy as I was. I couldn't even murmur something nice about Vince as a way to say something nice about the son I'd never met. I could have at least agreed Vince was handsome, but Vince forced his body into an athletic fitness that seemed as stiff and uncomfortable as my hollowed-out shell.

"Don't worry, love. I've been working on this for a while." Florence propped herself against the counter in her kitchenette, holding the neck of the wine bottle as though she might pour a drink into the glass she'd already refilled. "August fifteenth . . . mmm . . . four years and a little over two months ago."

I kept my eyes on Ernest and Julio Gallo's Chablis Blanc, the 1.5 liter green bottle with its thick neck strangled by tense fingers.

"He dressed up in my clothes and slit his wrists. He didn't even leave a fucking note. He simply wore my clothes to do it, and he wasn't into that, either; he wasn't kinky."

No wonder Florence was a washerwoman, a professional at removing stains and cleaning up messes on clothes. I thought of Lady Macbeth, washing and washing her hands.

She raised the bottle to pour herself another drink. She didn't see that she was about to overflow her glass, but rather seemed to notice the alarm in my eyes, and that caused her to set down the bottle with a thump. She bent to sip her drink without lifting the glass from the counter.

"Did you get any counseling, Florence?"

She straightened, glass in hand. "Oh, yes," she said bitterly. "My husband's paying for that. He insisted upon it. It's the only thing I accepted from the son-of-a-bitch. I think he was half glad, love. It gave him such a convenient excuse to leave me."

To my relief, someone knocked at the door.

"Come in, love," Florence called.

"I'm sorry, but I can't," Punky yelled through the door, talking fast.

Florence went to the door. Punky bounced on the step.

"I left Todd in the apartment, and I don't feel like I can be away from him for even two minutes, you know? I was wondering if you have Bobbi's phone number?"

"I don't know, love. I'll have to dig in all that crappola there." She pointed to the overflowing end table by her couch/bed.

"Well, if you can find it, would you please bring it down to me? I hate to ask that, but Todd's konked out, and that stuff last night has made me paranoid."

"Sure, love, but warn me if Bobbi is coming out, okay?"

Florence shut the door softly. "Poor thing." She took the candle from the refrigerator over to the end table and kneeled before the heap of papers and envelopes by the telephone. "I doubt if I have that number since I'd as soon none of those people ever came around. They never fix anything, anyway. Damn! I don't believe this!"

"What is it?"

"My son's gold cross is gone."

I eyed the junk heap skeptically, but said, "This is getting outrageous."

"It probably disappeared the same time as the money and I just never noticed 'til now."

"What kind of person would steal a cross?"

"Someone sick." Tears drizzled down her cheeks.

I had come to Florence's door seeking comfort, but I was slowly realizing all she had to offer was sorrow.

Dribbling Juice

By candlelight I dug in the drawer to my garage-sale desk, which the previous owner had been kind enough to deliver to my door. I had the manager's number. But, then, Punky hadn't asked me; Punky didn't know me. I paced the floor with the scrap of paper in my hand. My mechanical clock had stopped, but my biological clock said it was past my bedtime. I pulled back my new curtains and looked down the driveway at the other apartments. They looked as deserted and quiet as seashells. Prufrock came unbidden to me:

> *In a minute there is time*
> *For decisions and revisions which a minute will reverse.*

Why did I make everything so complicated? Why did I bang my head against the simplest decision, when in this age, one ill-advised second could undo everything anyway?

That is exactly the reason one should contemplate every action, I thought, but I had already pulled on my hooded sweatshirt and headed down the driveway.

Fully dressed and wary, Punky appeared at her door as though she had no plans to sleep. She held a candle in one hand and the darkness behind her poured forth marijuana fumes. She stood trembling in the autumn chill and didn't invite me in. After all, I was a teacher, and God knows how righteous teachers can be, and she was standing in that heavy, incriminating odor.

"I brought you the manager's phone number."

The instant I handed her the slip of paper, the world sprang to life. Light dazzled the room behind her, various apartments along the drive blinked on, a television, turned up too loud, broadcast into the night, and dogs barked at the sudden change. Power had been restored, but that didn't stop the sensation that it'd happened at our connection, like the anticipated explosion of light and energy when God's finger finally touched Adam's on the ceiling of the Sistine Chapel.

Punky thanked me for the number and blew out the now unnecessary candle, a pleasant vanilla fragrance curling up with the smoke.

"Are you going to be okay?" I asked.

She nodded. "In a couple of days I have to go somewhere, though." She shifted her weight and scratched at her cheek. "Do you think it would be okay to leave my boy with Mrs. Bean? She offered to watch him."

If I hadn't been so ignorant of children, if I'd thought more carefully about the question, I might not have said yes, and I might not have blamed myself for what happened. But that night, I was eager to give her something, and Mrs. Bean, with her sharp ears and vigilance, seemed like a safe bet.

The Soaps

The socs (popular, social students) in my junior classes were a group of white kids. Boys and girls alike dressed in a preppy style, polo shirts with the collars turned up. If it was cold, they threw on trim sweaters over the shirts. The boys sported short hair and Raybans and the girls tied back their hair in ribbons. They came from the more affluent families in the community, and although they had not been friendly to me, they were too well mannered to be vicious.

They had returned from the summer addicted to *Days of Our Lives*. As a snob who considered soaps a pastime for bored housewives with few alternatives, I needed months to catch on. I was used to kids in The City who wore tight clothes, smoked dope, and spent their weekends trying to sneak into clubs. It took me a while to grasp the buzz among these students consisted of daily fixes of this soap passed around from a student with a videocassette recorder.

Finally, after I'd asked Elene Petroutsas for the ump-teenth time to be quiet, she blurted, "But, Ms. Knutsen, I gotta find out what happened to Jessica Fallon."

"Who's Jessica Fallon?" I asked.

The class, even the non-socs, stared at me in astonishment.

While one student informed me Jessica Fallon was the illegitimate daughter of Alex Marshall, a hospital administrator, and his nurse Marie Curtis, and she had left town with Joshua

Fallon, I had the good sense to listen and not to pronounce judgment at the confusing list of soap characters. It was a turning point in my career. It may have been a turning point in my life.

On this foggy, chilly Friday, my brain teased me with questions worthy of a soap. Why wasn't Vince comforting Punky? Would Punky call the manager? Who was Lefty Hunt? Was he our thief?

How could I deny the appeal of such questions? Weren't they as stimulating as, "What effect does Poe create with his use of onomatopoeia in *The Bells*?"

I nervously glanced at the classroom clock, thinking about education classes and the prevailing omniscient god of educational theory: Time on Task.

We had ten minutes left. It was only October and I was exhausted. I could not go a whole year, pushing and pulling at these students, demanding attention they didn't want to give. Thirty-seven bodies sprawled before me—grown bodies, bodies that drove cars, made love, held jobs, consumed alcohol— bodies big enough to take some responsibility for whether they'd learn or not.

The desks hadn't changed much since I was in their place, plodding through Steinbeck's *The Grapes of Wrath*. One of my classmates had observed that if a guy spit, the dust rolled for three pages. As serious as I was about literature, even then, I had laughed. Because it was true. Not in a factual way. But in the way Faulkner meant when he said facts and truth really don't have much to do with each other.

I sighed audibly and perched on the side shelf of my lectern; it was the first time I'd sat in class. I rested my hands on the podium and noted with calm alarm the thinness of my fingers. They looked anorexic, starving.

I'd been quiet a full minute when I realized all thirty-seven bodies were deadly silent and staring at me with a certain amount of trepidation. I don't know what they feared, perhaps that I would faint, but behind the fear lay an element of guilt. They knew that if I did, they'd be partially responsible. This class had once thrown little bits of paper at me. It deserved to sweat. I took a second to be grateful Annette didn't sit at the back of this room. Of course, if she did, that fiasco probably never would have happened.

"Let me tell you about this guy who moved into the apartments where I live." I settled my butt a little more firmly onto the lectern shelf. "He's supposedly the son of an older couple who rented the place."

They were listening, all thirty-seven of them. After two months of constant struggle, suddenly, effortlessly, I had undivided attention from students who dismissed Jonathon Edwards as a fanatic, complained of Franklin's tediousness, and showed only a begrudging interest in Poe.

The class I'd thought of alternately as belligerent and apathetic was hanging raptly on each word. The moment was magic.

Same Time, Same Station

Florence knew the answers to most of my questions. Glad to put aside her *Psychology Today*, she held forth as I leaned against the warm, vibrating washer. The only chair in the laundry room was Florence's throne.

According to Florence, Punky would love to sleep with Vince, but she feared Lefty might report her again, claiming moral turpitude disqualified her as a parent.

"Seems like she'd be more afraid he'd call the police about the pot."

"Well, she's worried about that, too, but she also needs something to calm her down, love. She hasn't been sleeping at all. She's afraid Lefty will sneak into her apartment. Besides, Lefty isn't jealous of her marijuana."

"She thinks the motive is jealousy?"

"It's the only thing we could come up with."

I kept the idea of no motive to myself. "Did she call the manager about him?"

"That's the weird part, love. Bobbi says she did rent the place to an older couple, and they didn't say anything about a son. She's going to check on it."

I was surprised anyone had been able to reach Bobbi Headland. Then I reminded myself that life continued on Lostart Street after I left for work at six and before I returned at five. Clearly there were Bobbi sightings, I just wasn't home for them.

"I wouldn't want to be in Punky's shoes," I said.

"Well, love, that's only half of it. She's stuck there with that baby all day and doesn't know a soul down here except us. She has to go to the Unemployment Office on Monday."

If I'd kept my baby, would I be in the same position? Alone, facing the Unemployment Office, frightened? I doubted it. Angelo had always been generous, would have helped to provide for the baby, might even have married me if I'd kept it.

"She asked me if I thought it would be okay to leave Todd with Mrs. Bean," Florence continued, "since I guess old String offered to baby-sit."

"She asked me about Mrs. Bean, too. What did you say?"

"Well, you know, love, Mrs. Bean is awfully beat up."

"That's true."

"But I figured for a couple hours, what the hell. And you know, love, I think it'd do Old String Bean a world of good."

I smiled. That was a nice twist I hadn't thought of.

"Now, as if that girl didn't have enough troubles, one of those mice that Vince conned her into taking disappeared, and the other mouse is sick. It lies in the corner of the terrarium as if it will never move again."

"Maybe she should put it out of its misery."

"It's her kid's pet. Boy, I tell you, love, the only way she'd abuse that child is by loving him too hard."

The tone sounded confessional. Perhaps she'd smashed her own son with a ton of love.

The Language of Connection

The weekend dawned so lovely I slipped back to my original conception of the place as peaceful, even dull. The morning dampness burned off early, and, coffee in hand, I sat on my step to correct papers. The landing was big enough for a chair, but I only had two, my rocking chair and an upright that I shuffled between my typing table and my eating table.

Beside my step, a redwood bucket spilled pansies. When I was growing up, my mom nurtured pansies in a window box, a bright spot in our house. I would stare for long periods at their velvet colors—the sun yellow with blue centers blurring into sad symbols of the beauty my mom wanted, but never had.

Across the asphalt drive was The Invisible Lady's house. Although no one in the apartment complex went inside, The Invisible Lady had visitors. Most of them were in their thirties or forties. Some of them entered without knocking, so I assumed they were relatives or close friends. Maybe her children. They greeted me with pleasant "hellos" or "good mornings." Today, though, the place seemed deserted.

On Mrs. Bean's step, the door stood slightly ajar and Buddha Belly lolled in his position. He seemed like the world's laziest cat. I wondered if he'd ever even explored the opening in Mrs. Bean's floor. Probably, though, he couldn't fit his fat body through it.

I couldn't have asked for quieter neighbors, and, apparently,

Mrs. Bean, at least, felt lucky to have me, too. She'd slipped into the conversation several times how glad she was to have a sweet girl like me for her next-door neighbor and not somebody odd like that new boy in nine.

I glanced at the stack of papers in my lap and sighed. My freshmen were studying metaphors. So they'd written on what they'd be if they had to be inanimate objects. I read Rosaura's first. "I would be a mountain. Not just any old mountain. I'd be a powerful, majestic mountain like Everest so I could be there for people to admire. I'd stay there, in one place, with my head stuck up in the clouds feeling how good it is not to move. People would come from all over the world to see me."

I smiled. She'd even spelled majestic right.

Ruben's paper began, "I wood be a big old rock. Sometimes people think I'm a rock, anyway, so I would like to realy be a rock. Go in the WWF and crush my oponants."

This was pretty good for Ruben although he'd glanced over at Rosaura's paper and may have lifted his rock idea from her mountain. He'd asked me in class, "Ms. Knutsen, how do you spell bigol?"

"*Bigol?*"

"You know, like a bigol dog?"

My eyes blinked heavily, then I crouched down beside his desk and whispered, "Two words. Big. Old. B-I-G. O-L-D."

"You did well with Ruben," Annette said as I left the room. Later in the faculty lounge, as I pulled my sack lunch from the moldy refrigerator, she held the door open for me, and muttered, "Gonna get my bigol lunch." Then she laughed.

I rested my back against my apartment's stucco, trying to get comfortable on the landing. Each paragraph took only a minute to read, but I struggled over appropriate comments and then the grade. Their faces rose on the pages as I marked an F on the questioning, hurt eyes of a student who'd written an illegible half sentence, and I put an A on a cocky smile. It was too bad in a way that we couldn't grade attitudes. Personalities. Hearts.

"Your child writes beautifully, but he has a cruel, F personality."
"Your child struggles with English but she has an A+ heart."

If I'd had a child, what would future teachers write? A wave of gratitude, not to face that question, showered my body. I suspected that I would be like my least favorite parents, the ones who showed up at Back To School Night waiting for me to tell them their child was magnificent, who stood woodenly, staring into space, unable to hear anything resembling criticism.

Or a sad parent like my mom, with too many kids and too few dreams, stuck in a miserable town. The biggest fear of my life.

As I worked my way through the papers, Florence headed to the laundry room with a wicker basket full of clothing. Later Punky came out of her apartment and sat on her steps, while Todd, pulling a wooden duck on wheels, toddled around the driveway.

I waited for Lefty Hunt, but he never made an entrance, even when Vince came up the drive with a jar of orange juice and a morning paper and plopped on Punky's steps with her. In his shorts, tee shirt and sandals, he looked like a beach bum, all fire and air and light, while Punky smacked of San Francisco, of smoky coffee houses, and remnants of Haight-Ashbury combined with influences from all the social movements that had that strange, romantic city as their heart. Punky was dark like the night, round with water, mysterious as the moon.

Bucky followed Dudu up the driveway. Today Dudu vaunted a yellow, satiny bow. Bucky carried a piece of paper and appeared agitated, wiping at his brow over and over. The dog urinated at Mrs. Bean's lower step, but Mrs. Bean didn't fly out her door.

The prepubescent neighborhood boy returned to the drive to play catch with a friend, and I wagered how many papers I could finish before Mrs. Bean came out to yell at them. The thumping of their ball and the constant calls to one another annoyed me, and I wanted Mrs. Bean to chase them away. Although, with Halloween coming, she might be setting herself up.

"I'd be a door," the sweet Liliana wrote, "cuz a door can let things in and close things out."

"Why do they keep thending me these?" Bucky whined as Dudu peed on the water meter. He held the rectangle of paper to The Invisible Lady's screen. "Do they think I know theth people?"

I couldn't hear the answer. As he continued on his way, I saw he held one of those cards with an unclear black and white photo and the question, "Have you seen this person?"

The next paper was Jamie's. I pictured her—scrawny, sitting stooped, shoulders curling protectively around her heart. In class she squinted at the chalkboard, too embarrassed to wear her glasses. I would have moved her to the front, but she feared people behind her. She sensed them sniggering. She wished to be a valentine, so she could be picked out special and given with love.

The sun shone so brightly that the reflection from the paper hurt my eyes. The world seemed excruciatingly tender. If I were still a writer, what metaphor would I choose? Could I think of anything more poignant than these?

Halloween

Maybe I'd overdosed on the beauty of the weekend, but more likely I'd sampled too many of the caramels I'd made as a Halloween treat for my students. I woke up Monday morning, promptly vomited, and decided, new teacher or not, I'd better stay home. Copies of my seating charts and rosters were in my sub folder, and I would call in my lesson plans.

I was sitting in bed drinking peppermint tea, a hot water bottle on my tummy, when Punky dropped off Todd at Mrs. Bean's. Their conversation drifted through my window, Punky earnestly thanking Mrs. Bean, and Mrs. Bean protesting over and over, saying it would give her something to do, that she appreciated good neighbors, that it would be no trouble at all.

I dozed to the familiar, soothing neighborhood sounds.

I had no idea how long I'd been asleep when frantic pounding awakened me. Mrs. Bean stood on my landing without her wrap-around sunglasses. Tears trickled down her withered face. "Those people took that boy," she said in her regular, crotchety voice, belying the dewdrops. "I didn't think they could do it, but they did."

While we waited for Punky to come home from the Unemployment Office, I searched the phone book for Child Protective Services, gave them a ring, and requested directions to the office. I pressed Mrs. Bean into my rocking chair. Sick or not, I would drive and get involved in this mess.

I'd been learning at school. Do a favor for a favor. You scratch my back and I'll scratch yours. The sayings were simply coarser forms of The Golden Rule. If I wanted people to care whether I was well or ill, or whether I had light during a post-earthquake blackout, I might first have to care about them, to share myself. Besides, Punky was even less familiar with the area than I was. Furthermore, I'd recommended Mrs. Bean.

As I washed and dressed, a nauseous haze muffled Mrs. Bean's incessant blaming of herself. "I don't know how that boy got that pack of matches," she muttered. "I don't use matches," she declared. "I thought it was another one of Lefty Hunt's doings, but when I tried to explain about him, they thought I was nuts."

While I poured tea for both of us, she rocked viciously, my poor chair creaking wildly even under Mrs. Bean's slight weight.

"Then, after they left," her voice turned sorrowful, "I remembered Florence lighting the wick of my lamp for me."

Punky finally arrived. The ride to the building of the Child Protective Services was like being trapped in a horror scene of a Halloween film. Punky interspersed crying and blaming herself with choice epithets for Lefty, and Mrs. Bean, who I had not wanted to come, moaned and reprimanded herself in a harsher, but weaker, voice than she used on any neighborhood boy.

I thought of the things people say to comfort others.

"Don't worry. Everything will be okay," Angelo had said when I'd discovered my pregnancy. The hackneyed phrases seemed like lies. Denial. Avoidance. Not something I would offer anyone.

Punky's unmollified rage mounted toward hysteria. Her fury whipped around in my Volkswagen bug like a spirit, and Mrs. Bean's soul faded like a ghost slipping to a cooler clime.

Emeline Street had its own exit from the freeway, a short decline into a residential neighborhood. I panicked. This could not possibly be the way to county officialdom. I stretched my neck both ways searching for a clue.

"To the right," Mrs. Bean croaked.

The Climax

Emeline Street dead-ended with a stand of eucalyptus to the left and a maze of buff-colored, two-storied county buildings to the right. By luck, I drove us right to the front of Building 1040, the address listed in the phone book. Signs identified the two entrances "Employment and Training" and "Human Resources Agency."

Human Resources seemed the more likely despite the opaqueness of the term. Believing that anyone who saw us entering the building must know the accusation, the alleged crime that brought us here, and that this imaginary audience must rank child abusers as I did, on par with rapists of old ladies, I blushed as we walked up the stately brick steps.

We were all silent.

The office with its bland tan walls and frayed magazines sucked the remaining life out of us. Even Mrs. Bean's eczema blanched and she keeled more than usual toward her bent leg.

A matronly woman with purple-gray, beauty parlor hair looked up at us from the service window.

"Where is Child Protective Services?" I asked.

"Right here." Her alert eyes took us in without any apparent hostility.

"My child is here," Punky said.

Even in all her agitation, Punky seemed to realize that yelling would complicate and confuse matters as well as possibly convince someone that she was, indeed, capable of child abuse. "Todd Hayes. He's two years old."

"He's not exactly here," the woman said.

"What?" Punky yelped. "Where is he then?"

The phone rang. "Excuse me," the woman said. She swiveled in her chair.

Punky stared anxiously through the window as though she could mentally transport the matron to a conclusion with the person on the phone.

I could tell by the woman's low, restrained voice that the caller was also upset. What a job, I thought. I helped Mrs. Bean to a chair.

When the lady finished, Punky assailed her. "Where is he? Is he all right? Can I have him?"

"I know this is frustrating for you, Mrs. Hayes, but you'll have to wait until a worker can interview you. Many children are released to their parents' custody, but some are not."

"You mean they might keep Todd?" For all her animal pain and anger, Punky clearly had not considered this possibility. She knew she was innocent. Punky looked up at me with gray eyes that begged for reassurance.

I couldn't find it in myself to tell her everything would be fine, because I had absolutely no idea what would happen. I did much better when I had the distance and space to write a note of consolation. Then I could fall back on my favorite Emily Dickinson poem:

> *"Hope" is the thing with feathers--*
> *That perches in my soul--*

Later I congratulated myself for not reciting the poem to Punky. Instead, I leaned over and awkwardly put an arm around her and patted her shoulder three times.

I'd always found Dickinson's poem a comfort, since it focused on how Hope remained, asking only a crumb, but the very metaphor of a bird suggested Hope could fly away. A precarious, flighty thing.

"I don't know the particulars of your case, Mrs. Hayes, but I imagine Todd will be released to you," the woman said. She was as ordinary as any old woman you might see stepping from a church after a Sunday service—neat, well-groomed, with her earrings and necklace matching and her dress a simple cut and floral print, a bit like Barbara Bush, but at second glance, she appeared a sage, regarding us with calm blue-green eyes. They did not rake over us as though we could be baby beaters, but rather seemed to suggest that everything would be okay. "I'll see if Mr. Gutierrez is ready to see you." She rose from her chair.

Within a minute, the little man peeped through the service window at us. "Ah, we meet again," he said melodramatically to Punky.

He didn't object to my presence with Punky, but he asked that Mrs. Bean remain in the waiting room. We followed him to his office and sat across the desk from him while Mr. Gutierrez nicely, but firmly, reminded Punky of the prior police report which had contributed to their decision to take Todd into custody, in spite of the fact they'd seen nothing on the "previous occasion."

"But a crazy guy made that report," Punky protested. She explained about Lefty Hunt, and I tried to back her up, but even as we talked, it sounded like an implausible story. The suspect lacked motivation.

"And do you assume the same guy made this call?"

Punky and I exchanged surprised looks. None of us had known there was a call.

"I suppose you thought I was just in the neighborhood," he said sarcastically. "You should take the matter of this guy up with the police. As you've been told, we don't ask callers to identify themselves, so we have no way to verify your account. Asking for identification would scare away too many legitimate tips."

We nodded in unison like a pair of Bobble heads.

"Now," Mr. Gutierrez said, laying his hands on his cluttered metal desk, "the second reason for our decision, Ms. Hayes, is that your child was not left in proper care."

Punky looked at her lap. "I don't know anyone here and Mrs. Bean offered to take Todd, just for a couple hours, while I went to the Unemployment Office."

Luckily Punky's eyes, cast down in shame, didn't witness the dance of the man's eyebrows when she mentioned unemployment. Bile rose in my throat like I might vomit again. I wouldn't have minded heaving right onto Mr. Gutierrez's stacks of forms if I hadn't thought it would jeopardize Punky's case. I swallowed hard.

"I understand your situation, Ms. Hayes, but in two hours anything can happen. Your child was found with a pack of matches in his hand, and Mrs. Bean didn't even know he had them. If he'd started a fire, would she have been able to put it out? Would she even be able to get help? Surely you can't argue this woman was an appropriate caregiver."

Punky's head dipped another half inch as I silently allowed this crucifixion for carelessness in which I shared culpability.

Mrs. Bean was asleep in the chair when we emerged from Mr. Gutierrez's office. He'd made a call to a foster home, and we sat in the waiting room with the snoring Mrs. Bean until a sturdy woman with graying hair marched through the door with Todd riding on her hip. A clumsy exchange followed, the foster parent reserved and distrusting, Punky humiliated and slightly hostile, Todd alert and not at all traumatized, simply interested in all these new twists to life.

At the touch of my hand, Mrs. Bean startled and immediately apologized for snoozing. We fled the building with Punky squeezing Todd so fiercely in her arms that the child squirmed and fidgeted.

The trip home was somber, the air laden with guilt. Mrs. Bean scolded herself for allowing the authorities to take the boy. I hated myself for recommending Mrs. Bean in the first place and for not better defending Punky in the office.

The hot air in the car pressed on us. My skin felt like a container, my lips clamped against communication. Sweat trickled from my fevered forehead and dripped down the inside of my T-shirt. I'd dressed in such a daze, I couldn't remember if I'd combed my hair.

Wanting desperately to take a shower and a nap, I dropped off Punky and Todd and Mrs. Bean with barely civil good-byes. I also had to call the school to tell them I wouldn't need the sub again tomorrow. Staying home was way too complicated.

A Ticker Tocks

Mrs. Bean hunched on her steps, staring down the asphalt drive as though gazing into eternity, the big, lumpy mass of Buddha Belly cradled on her lap.

Bucky, out for the evening ritual with Dudu, spotted the forlorn Mrs. Bean. Dudu, for all his sentimental cuteness and ribbons, marched with Napoleonic firmness right up to piss at the railing of the old woman's steps. But Mrs. Bean's filmy eyes remained glued to nothingness. Thus, Bucky, unable to write more than vital statistics taught to him by rote, squatted down before the old woman to take on the burden of her grief.

"Whath the matter, Mrs. Bean?" he asked.

"My Buttons is dead." One eczema-ridden hand cupped the large head and the other stroked the long hair of the precious Himalayan as the woman gazed into space. Every law of physics said the dead weight should slide from her spindly lap, whapping the concrete step and wrenching the head from Mrs. Bean's embrace. But, a small miracle fastened the unwieldy body to the fragile legs.

"I don't understand the people who live here." The ratchety reproach grated through Cecile's window and woke her. "I've lived here for twenty years. People here know me. They know I live back here by myself, that I can't get around, and no one stops to say hello or to have a cup of coffee." Her grief became less spiky and more generalized. Like a lumpy, failed pudding. "I don't understand this world anymore."

Paradox at the Center of My Heart

Outside my apartment, Mrs. Bean cried for comfort, but I was sticky with fever. The next morning I would have to face work and the chaos left by a substitute. And I'd already spent the day hauling her and Punky to the county offices.

So I kept my lights off and pretended to be asleep, hiding from Mrs. Bean's grief and any trick-or-treaters. If Mrs. Bean weren't such a crab, I rationalized, more people would visit her. Besides, who understood the world anyway?

The barracks didn't attract many children, but a few shuffled past, hesitating at the darkness of my apartment, and then going on to shout "trick-or-treat" at Mrs. Bean. I imagined her treats. Old pieces of hard candy stuck to their cellophane wrappers. And then she'd expect a gracious, "Thank you."

I tossed and turned until well after midnight, plagued by Mrs. Bean's invective and images of papers overflowing from my desk and turning into autumn leaves that scuttled across the body of a dead, fat cat.

Florence's Conviction

When I woke in the morning I said "rabbits" before anything else so I would have good luck in November.

Before school started, Rosaura found me in Annette's classroom hastily chalking our agenda on the board.

"Ms. Knutsen," she asked, "are you anorexic?"

I turned to face her with the bizarre feeling she knew I'd spent the previous day vomiting. I liked her, but she was such a nervy girl. She was nothing more than a child's stick figure herself—no breasts to speak of and wild loops of hair on top her head.

"No," I said crisply, "I am not."

"Okay, then. I brought you a churro."

She stepped closer and handed me a crisp white bakery bag dotted with grease. This gift from a girl who wore the same pair of jeans every day.

"Thank you, Rosaura." My heart hurt like it had been stabbed. "How thoughtful of you."

Rosaura waited, her Converse sneakers planted on the dirty linoleum. She glanced at the bag and then at my mouth.

Apparently I needed to prove I didn't have an eating disorder. I extracted the long slender doughnut, sugar sprinkling the floor. Positioning my mouth over the white bag, I took a bite.

"*Sabrosa.*" Delicious. It was.

The doughnut and Rosaura's kindness got me through that day at school. I felt floaty and disconnected. In the middle of explaining compare-and-contrast essays to the freshmen, I forgot what I was talking about, slowly erased the board while I tried to remember, and finally simply asked them to compare this Halloween to last Halloween in their journals. I gave the juniors an impossible reading assignment and threatened them with detentions if they talked.

"You're tired, huh?" Elene Petroutsas said.

I didn't ask her how she knew.

After school, in spite of my stacks of papers, I stopped by Florence's for my fix of gossip. I rapped a shave-and-a-haircut on her weathered door.

"Who is it?" Her words already sounded slurred.

"Me."

"Who is me?"

"Cecile." How could she not recognize my voice?

"Come in."

Florence slumped to the side in one of the rattan chairs drawn up to the television. Her hand dangled toward a water glass of wine. The television worked now, but she stared at it in an annoyed way as if it were out of focus. "Sorry," she said, "but us women living alone, we can't be too careful, love."

Since she'd answered the door before, I wondered if the Lefty Hunt business was getting to her. Or, perhaps she was worried I might be Bobbi, or maybe she couldn't get out of the chair.

She flapped a hand for me to take the other rattan chair, so I brushed the calico cat off it and pulled my seat closer to hers.

She turned her blurry eyes toward me. "Can I offer you a drink?"

"I'll get it." I sprang up before she had a chance to try.

"I suppose you know Buddha Belly died," she said as I rounded the corner to the kitchenette.

I was glad to be out of sight. "Yeah."

"He got buried today," she said as I settled into the chair again and promptly sneezed from the stirred up cat hair. "Bless you."

"Where was he buried?"

"In one of those animal cemeteries. I took old Mrs. Bean down there today. She had the cat bundled in a piece of black velvet with a plastic red rose across the top."

After a long pause during which the television newswoman told of a murder and a traffic accident, Florence declared with surprising clarity and firmness, "We have to get her another cat."

The November 2 Episode of "Love on Lostart"

Vince saw Punky peeking at him through the window. She flung open the door, grabbed a handful of shirt, and tugged him through the door into the apartment.

"We've got to stop meeting like this," he said, instantly wishing he could be more original, but feeling happy that she was glad to see him. He'd finally done his laundry (for the last two days he'd gone to work without any underwear), but Florence seemed to have forgotten all about the catnapping. She'd filled his ear with info about Todd and Child Protective Services.

Lefty Hunt's threats were serious and prompted apparently by jealousy of him. Vince had considered staying away from Punky to make her life easier and realized that he didn't want to.

Punky rested her head against his chest and he tightened, but then he placed a hand in the dip between the wings of her back. He smiled weakly into the dusky hair under his nose and marveled at how small she felt even though she was chubby.

"I'm glad you're here," she said as she pulled away from him. She filled in the details of the trip to Child Protective Services.

"Jesus," he said, "that guy's loony. Did you call the manager again?"

Punky put the copper kettle on the stove. "Bobbi knows about Lefty, but it can take three months to evict a person and there has to be a reason."

She moved like liquid, Vince thought, as Punky went on. They had no proof Lefty had made the calls, but she might be able to involve the police on grounds of harassment.

"I have a surprise for you." Punky held up in succession a brown bag of freshly ground coffee, a plastic funnel and then a package of one-cup filters. When she measured out a scoop of coffee and poured hot water over it, the rich aroma curled into the room.

"Wow," he said. "Thank you." He felt like a king. A pleasant contrast to being regarded as a lowly warehouse worker.

Taking the mug of coffee, he folded down onto his futon throne. Todd was pushing a yellow, rubber tractor between straddled legs, blowing air through his lips.

With a cup of tea in hand, Punky followed him down to the futon. "I wonder if I could ask you a big favor."

The coffee lost some of its deliciousness.

"Could you keep my pot plant for a few days." She spread her eyes wide to show her openness. "In case I have to call the police."

The words probed like a queen's pawn opening. The whole game depended on his response.

His doubt dissolved into the grayness of her eyes. "Sure."

"I know this is asking a lot." She waited, giving him time to retract.

Vince sipped the coffee. He would not change a move after he'd taken his hand from a piece. "This is good shit," he said about the coffee.

That night, after the child was asleep, they lay on the futons together. His heart thumped and he knew she must feel it, the way he felt her warmth seeping through his clothing. He kissed her forehead, down her nose to her lips. She wrapped soft arms around his neck and pulled him against the cushiony breasts and he wondered why he'd always preferred bony girls. Society must have taught him that, and here he considered himself so impartial, so fair, so rational.

He thought of the license plate holder on the back of The Fat Lady's red mustang that said: TRY FAT AND YOU'LL NEVER GO BACK. He had snorted at it. No way. Rolls of fat were ugly, obscene, unhealthy. Now he doubted himself. He felt as though he were sinking.

He abruptly propped himself on his elbows and forced his mind to face facts, to become hard and clear. The lazy protest humming from her distracted him. Her eyes were closed, her face fluttered in the candlelight, and rich muskiness undulated under his nose. He remained rigid until her eyelids lifted.

"Do you take the pill?" he asked.

"Don't worry," she said.

He sank back to the futon and her hand ran down the front of his shirt, catching and releasing buttons. A finger traced his ribs.

He moved his hands under the yoga top and encountered no bra, just flesh, pliable as bread dough, but then he jerked away, and she opened her eyes again.

"Diaphragm?" The word rolled clumsily from his tongue.

"Rhythm," she whispered seductively.

He sat all the way up. "Russian roulette."

She sighed and sat up, too.

"I'm not into making babies," he said.

She propped her chin in her hand. "Do you think I am?"

"Is that how you got him?" He nodded toward the bedroom door. "Using rhythm?"

"No. We used nothing. We simply gave in to the occasion." Her voice had a bit of bite in it.

He touched the glimmering mass of hair, but she recoiled.

"I know my rhythms." Her voice now sounded hurt and angry, a tone he'd never heard her use before.

"I believe you."

"I don't think you do," she said.

He caressed the face flittering in the candlelight, but she

tucked her head against her shoulder as if his fingers were violating her. "I do," he said gently.

She pressed her face against his bare chest and he stroked her hair. "I'm sorry," he said.

"It's too late."

Tiny spots of dampness tingled his chest.

Later, when she'd blown out the candles, she told him she had pre-menstrual blues, but that didn't change the fact another night passed without sex.

In the wee hours, they got cold and moved to the bed, rolling Todd to the edge. At times like this she wondered what she would do as Todd grew older and they would need a bigger apartment. Maybe they'd be forced to live in some crummy place or she would have to turn to her parents and feel, no matter how pleasantly they offered assistance, that they gloated in smugness. *Told you so.*

She snuggled close to Vince's sinewy body. When she awoke, the bed was empty beside her and she groped across the space for Todd. Where he'd lain, the wet mattress reeked of ammonia. She squeezed her eyes shut, slammed her fist on the mattress, and laughed, wondering how Vince responded to a wet bed.

On the kitchen counter the key to his apartment reposed like a stamen in the heart of a small white paper curled up at the edges. The note said to go ahead and move the plant and was signed "love, Vince." Tenderness flooded her. Some men might have been bitter or nasty after an evening like the one they'd had. And Vince had probably thought for a while before choosing that word; he wasn't the type to use "love" carelessly.

Todd was pushing Cheerios through the screen to the sick mouse. She couldn't afford a vet fee for a stupid mouse, and each day Punky half hoped to find it dead, but Love proved tenacious. Punky let the child play in his pajamas while she dressed and prepared to tackle the problem of the plant.

Scouting the area, Punky propped open both the door to Vince's apartment and the door to her own, covered the plant with a sheet, and staying turned toward Lefty's door, lugged the pot to Vince's apartment. With both the shades and curtains drawn, she maneuvered the plant past the dim outlines of furniture to the back bedroom where a fish tank gurgled and hummed.

As her eyes adjusted to the dark, she absorbed the orderly bedroom, the neatly-made, simple, steel-framed bed. A calendar and a bulletin board hung on the wall, but no paintings or prints. With the exception of the terrarium and aquarium, everything seemed functional. No extra pillows topped the bed; no photos graced the rectangular, four drawer dresser.

A squeal hurled through the wall at her. Punky sprinted to the driveway. Lefty Hunt slid out the door of her apartment, dragging Todd by the wrist.

The child writhed and squirmed. "Mamamama!"

She ran toward them. "What are you doing with my child? That's kidnapping. A felony!"

The Bible appeared from behind Lefty's back and rose over his head. She halted a few steps in front of him.

Lefty smiled.

The desolation of the place seeped into her consciousness. Vince was at work; Cecile was teaching. The laundry room stood empty as Florence slept off her nightly bout. The Fat Lady didn't come home until midmorning. A shout for help might only upset Lefty and reach no one.

"Why are you doing this to me?" she asked.

Lefty stared, grinning, but holding the Bible high as though it were an offering and cinching his other hand so tightly around Todd's wrist that the skin puckered under the fingers. Todd whimpered and tried to pull away by dropping to his knees, his face beseeching Punky to rescue him.

"You're scaring us," she said. "Is that what you want?"

"He's the devil!" Lefty shouted, and then soothingly he said, "We're all left-handers."

"Let me have my baby."

Lefty released Todd's arm and touched the child's head. "See how the whorl of his hair goes counterclockwise?"

Freed, Todd ran to Punky and she swept him up.

"Leonardo da Vinci, Michelangelo, Joan of Arc, Picasso, Ben Franklin, you and me." Lefty whirled. "Stay away from him. Stay away from that man!" Lefty stalked across the driveway toward his apartment, and Punky hurried to her unit to call the police.

That morning, Vince had decided that all the mice in his car had crawled into the bottle and were trapped there. After work, he'd drop them off at a pet store where they could be used as snake food.

When he arrived at work, the receptionist said, "You look nice," as though she didn't notice he wore the same shirt as he had the day before and that he smelled slightly of pee. "You look like someone who's captured the mouse market," she teased.

He did feel buoyant. He had lain beside Punky until the last minute, debating whether to call in sick, and when he'd decided to go, he didn't have time to shower, but it didn't matter. He didn't believe for a moment that love conquered all. But it conquered a whiff of urine.

The Tocker Ticks

As Lefty dragged Todd from the apartment, Florence was not sleeping one off. She was absent from the laundry room because she was preparing to relinquish her calico cat for the soul of Mrs. Bean. She waited until the old lady would be up, and then gathered the motley mass in her arms. Hair coated her hands as Florence stroked and caressed the cat, murmuring good-byes and comforting herself that the cat would be nearby.

She explained to the cat that she'd have a new home. Florence had dismissed the idea of Tom, her favorite, and the other two were too wild to adjust to the sedentary life at Mrs. Bean's. Florence prayed old String would pamper the cat as she had Buddha Belly. The sacrifice had to be made and this neurotic cat called Cowlickcoo that loved to loaf in any hot spot was the best choice. She could hardly afford to buy the woman a new Himalayan, but without a companion, Mrs. Bean would not live long. Florence felt sure of that.

As Florence knocked and knocked at Mrs. Bean's door, the cat became more aroused and frightened, until finally Florence, who'd known Mrs. Bean for ten years, called, "It's me, love," and cracked the front door.

Springing from Florence's arms, the calico cat landed on the lap of pale pink, synthetic fiber with two toothpick legs protruding from it, and from there to the floor.

"Didn't you hear me at the door?" Florence said.

Undisturbed by the wild cat and enveloped by an over-stuffed chair, the old woman stretched her eyes wide and clasped what used to be her bosom. "Oh, yes," she moaned, "but I'm having a heart attack, Florence."

With the experience of a woman who for fifty years had attracted catastrophes, Florence picked up the phone, but before dialing, she peeked out the window. To her disbelief, as though God were in Heaven and still performed miracles, a Sheriff's vehicle rolled into the driveway.

With nervous glances toward Lefty's unit, Punky watched the arrival of the cruiser from the Sheriff's Office through the window. This small, unincorporated neighborhood didn't even have a police department, and the green sheriff's car with the gold star on the door arrived without a siren. She'd imagined a more dramatic rescue.

She drew back from the window, almost knocking over Todd who'd been clinging to her leg since the incident. With a palm on each of the boy's healthy cheeks, she manipulated his head looking for boogers, earwax, dirt, and other natural child phenomena that might be construed as neglect. She double checked her own hair in the bathroom mirror and tried to imagine the first impression of her apartment on this sheriff deputy.

When enough time had passed so that even the greenest of horns should have made it to the door, she glanced out the window again. The ephemeral car had vaporized. Inculcated with the magic of Irish folklore, enchanted by acid trips as a teenager, and receptive as an adult to the mysterious, when Punky peered down the drive and still didn't see anything, she consulted her *Guide to Alternatives to Chemical Medicine* for a calming blend of herbs. Had she hallucinated?

As she put the teakettle on the stove, the trauma of the morning caught up with Todd. He wailed, tugging at the hem of her shirt, wanting to be picked up, crying for his binky, the immediate demands driving out Punky's thought of calling the sheriff again.

The Invisible Lady

A book bag weighed down my right arm, the hand grasping a huge ring of keys. My purse, my empty lunch bag, and a ten-pound American literature text that I couldn't squeeze into the book bag encumbered the other arm. I liked the challenge of trying to pick up my mail and open the front door without unloading anything. This feat required clutching something either with my knees or teeth, and I'd just stuck the corners of the junk mail into my mouth so my fingertips could handle the keys, when behind me a clear, healthy, unmistakably feminine voice said, "Come here. I want to meet you."

I barely turned, believing no one would compromise me in such an awkward position, but then the voice directed me, "Over here." My ears told me the sound came from The Invisible Lady's apartment, but that seemed so unlikely my gaze roved the driveway for a woman.

I cracked my door and lowered the bag inside the front room, took the mail from my mouth and peered around again for the owner of the voice.

"Come to the window," the voice said.

The young voice probably belonged to one of The Invisible Lady's relatives. I dumped the rest of my things into my apartment and walked across the asphalt to the window.

Although declining into dusk, the November afternoon still glowed brighter than the inside of the apartment so I could see only a silhouette with flowing locks that spilled over squared shoulders. Since the apartments were raised from the asphalt, my head cocked at an uncomfortable angle as I squinted through the screen at the woman who seemed to be separated from the window by a table or desk.

"Aren't you cold with the window open?" I asked in my motherly, school-teacher way.

"Oh, I wear a sweater to watch the world," she said lightly. "Besides I might ask you the same question."

"There's a gas leak in my apartment."

The woman sighed impatiently. "Good grief. Why don't you call P.G. & E?"

"I thought I had to check with the landlord first." This had to be The Invisible Lady, but I'd expected a poor, helpless creature. An elderly person. I didn't think it polite to ask why she didn't come out, what her affliction might be, so I waited for her to reveal her purpose. She reached across her desk, unfastened the bottom of her screen, and nudged it outward. Slender, elegant, white fingers extended from the crack with a white paper folded like a business letter. This hand belonged to a young person. I leaned closer and saw that the flowing reddish hair framed a smooth face, the face of a woman neither young nor old.

"Since you're a member of the world's most important profession," she said without the slightest trace of irony, "I thought you might appreciate this."

One had merely to suggest I might like something to guarantee I'd dislike it. I started to unfold the paper.

"No," she said, "read it at home over your afternoon coffee where you don't feel pressure to respond."

"Well, thanks," I said uncertainly. That she knew I was a teacher didn't bother me. That seemed obvious enough, but I found it a trifle disconcerting that she knew my habit of contemplating matters over afternoon coffee. As a matter of fact, it piqued me since I knew nothing about her. I didn't even know if she was The Invisible Lady for certain. I didn't like people to be one up on me, although I couldn't blame anyone but myself, the way I holed up with my schoolwork.

I saved the mysterious paper until I'd situated myself at my desk with a cup of serious brew. I opened the flaps. After the small, scrawling cursive of my students, the enlarged print was inviting:

PURPOSE OF EDUCATION

I am a survivor of a concentration camp. My eyes saw what no person should witness. Gas chambers built by learned engineers. Children poisoned by educated physicians. Infants killed by high school and college graduates. So I'm suspicious of education. My request is: help your students to be human. Your efforts must never produce learned monsters, skilled psychopaths, or educated Eichmanns. Reading and writing and spelling and history and arithmetic are only important if they serve to make our students human.

Yes, I thought, this touched my first principles of education, but the paragraph also puzzled me. Who'd written it? The woman I'd seen looked too young to be a concentration camp survivor. I wondered why she had given it to me. Was she trying to tell me something? Did she think I was producing Eichmanns?

At the bottom, she'd written a short note in dark, bold pencil: "Have you been robbed, yet? The thief went through my medicine cabinet, but didn't find anything worth using or very marketable.

P.S. Mrs. Bean had a heart attack. Florence took her to the hospital."

I rubbed my temples. If I hadn't put Mrs. Bean through the ordeal with Todd, if I'd offered comfort when Buddha Belly died, maybe this would not have happened.

To fortify myself, I sipped the coffee. I reread the other

part of her note. The Invisible Lady had been robbed, too. I had thought she was always home. Either I was wrong about that, or our thief was really bold. This theft, like the others, looked like an inside job—someone who, unlike me, would know when The Invisible Lady left her apartment. The note stated "the thief," one thief, and I wondered whom, among us, that could be. Certainly not The Fat Lady, Mrs. Bean, or Bucky. Well, why not The Fat Lady? What did I really know about her? Why not Bucky? Just because he was slow?

My missing sweater wouldn't fit either of them, but whoever took it could hardly wear it around the complex anyway. The thief had ransacked The Invisible Lady's medicine cabinet. *Looking for drugs?* I hated to think it, but Florence was a definite substance abuser. She had been robbed, too, but really, I had only her word on that. And Florence had gone out of her way not to involve anyone in investigating the burglaries.

Lefty Hunt seemed like the best suspect, but Mrs. Bean's diamonds had disappeared before he and Punky arrived.

It was important to nail this person. Not because of the thefts, but because suspicion could destroy our community.

Speculations on The Invisible Lady

I never asked anyone about The Invisible Lady. All the questions I formed seemed impertinent. I did not have the social grace of small talk, and to attack the matter without preliminary patter would offend people. So, I fantasized.

The Invisible Lady took on shades of Emily Dickinson, not the romantic spurned lover dressed in white or the kooky eccentric, but the intense personality who wrote, "If I feel physically as if the top of my head were taken off, I know that is poetry." Emily's intensity drained people, and maybe The Invisible Lady was the same, retreating from the world, watching us from a distance to shield us from her penetrating eyes and demanding depth.

In my mind, The Invisible Lady became a writer who had composed the note she slipped to me. She knew such thoughts were not for ordinary conversation. Behind her window, she observed our triteness and chuckled at our banality while celebrating the vitality and ecstasy she chose not to inflict upon us.

She Doesn't Smell Like a Beach Bunny

As Vince drove home that Thursday, his lust dissipated into an occasional throb of the groin. The faint scent of urine scrambled his brain, as only scents can do. This woman has a baby, the smell told him, but, at the very same moment, it evoked her bed and the softness of her breasts against his back.

He had considered a vasectomy more than once, but that seemed so permanent. Maybe, some day, he'd want a kid, but for now, he loved his freedom to drive home from work, throw on his beach shorts, and go to Rio Del Mar for a long run, or to Santa Cruz Main Beach for a game of volleyball, or maybe to Manresa to surf even though he wasn't a good surfer. He didn't have to think about dinner if he didn't want to, much less a baby-sitter, or an infant sick with all those things they get— measles and mumps and chicken pox and colic.

How could he have been so stupid? To be in bed with a woman with a baby.

Then he'd get a whiff of his shirt and everything would go haywire again until logic beat a stubborn path through the chaos.

He wasn't attached, yet. He hadn't made her any promises, given her any ring, or claimed he loved her. Just the little *love* on the note. Of course, it would be awkward with her living next door, but he'd break it off now, before any real damage. They could be friends.

Shit, he thought, maybe she wasn't even looking for a serious relationship. She probably had other lovers. He worried too much. He was too fucking responsible. Relax, he told himself. Enjoy it.

Punky tried to read Todd *The Three Little Pigs*, but the Big Bad Wolf kept becoming Lefty Hunt, and she was the first little pig with the house of straw. If she'd kept her act together, they'd be living in a better place, but here she was disgracefully unemployed, suspected of child abuse because of a nut, and with no options but to run to someone. She'd never read the fable with so much sympathy for the first little pig. The Big Bad Wolf huffed and puffed right into her heart so it exploded along with the straw house and she understood emotionally the socio-economic implications that whirled across the pages with all those bits of the cheaply, poorly made house of piglet *numero uno*.

When Punky answered the door, her crooked smile and her gray eyes so glad to see him, and the thick, fragrant hair floating around her like an aura, Vince's resolve to end "it" dissolved. When she kissed him, his knees weakened, and his cock swelled.

They spent the evening kissing, hugging, talking, groping, shedding clothes, and wishing Todd would go to sleep. Punky was wearing lacy black panties, and Vince was thrilled. Whether she wore sexy underwear all the time or had put them on for him, both were good. Lust triumphantly conquered fear of commitment and fear of the Big Bad Wolf.

The covers finally tucked about the boy, Vince and Punky retired to the living room floor. She lit a candle. Although he was hard, she caressed his face, stroked his body, pinched his nipples, and kissed her way to his erection, which she circled with the tip of her tongue. Her rhythm was one of leisure and he thought he'd erupt.

Vince scooped her into his arms and flipped her under him.

As he entered her, the olfactory system pumped its information directly to the limbic regions of the brain, and the primitive sense of smell, the only sense that bypassed his overactive thalamus, told him Punky was his first woman who didn't smell like suntan lotion.

A Chapter for Lefty

Lefty Hunt took a butcher knife from his kitchen drawer because he'd been commanded to do so. He had been hearing a voice ever since he'd gotten confused about his meds. At first he thought a spirit lived in the apartment and he searched for it, but gradually he had realized that God was talking to him again. It had to be God. Who else could it be?

Lefty Hunt had been an autumn child. His brother and sister were almost old enough to be his parents. His mother, Louise, channeled all her intellect toward creative ways to support her rigorous, fundamentalist upbringing, and his father, William, Sr., was the stereotype of the henpecked husband.

Lefty had passed for normal all through high school, although people, in retrospect, could pick out oddities. He excelled in science and was a lanky, average-looking kid, but he had few friends and no girlfriends. He told inane stories with no points and laughed at them even when others were annoyed or impatient. Still, this only earned him a reputation as weird, not crazy. His classmates and teachers who bothered to think about Lefty's emotional immaturity blamed it on his mom, who emphatically professed everyone should be a virgin until married. It didn't bother her a whit that Lefty had no apparent interest in popularity or the opposite sex.

When Lefty decided to attend a fundamentalist bible

college, she was ecstatic, and when he began to hear the voice of God, she held him in awe. Yet, a tiny part of her not dominated by religious fervor noted that her son was becoming more and more slovenly. He let his hair grow into a straggly mop and no matter how she urged him to bring home his laundry, he went about in an increasingly disreputable state.

Even when Lefty's personal neglect led to his dismissal from a fast food restaurant and prompted William, Sr. to say mildly at the dinner table, "Something's wrong with that boy," Louise became livid, comparing her son's long hair to that of Christ, and defending his poor personal hygiene as a sign of his lack of ego, his humility.

Lefty's condition deteriorated for several years until the day he stood on a speaker's dais at the center of the college's green claiming he was a messiah come to liberate left-handers and to expose devils. In a community predisposed to believe in the wonders and strange ways of God, Lefty probably could have gotten away with the sermon if he hadn't decided on that day to forget about his clothes altogether.

To his mother's way of thinking, Lefty was like St. Francis of Assisi. People had called Francis crazy when he had shed his clothes and given them to beggars, and that is what they called Lefty.

After he was 5150ed, the more concerned people at the college noted that "Lefty didn't use to be that way." Lefty entered a psychiatric ward for evaluation. The doctor there, quite aware of his colleagues' over-diagnosis of schizophrenia, cautiously considered the DSM III criteria for the illness and then called Lefty's problem a Schizoaffective Disorder. Louise referred to Lefty's illness as her "cross to carry" although she agreed quite readily to institutionalization. She was, after all, sixty-two years old. She had neither the energy nor knowledge the doctors possessed. She would, and did, pray for her son.

William, Sr. simply didn't mention the subject except to tell his wife he'd prefer not to have the bumper sticker, but she still stuck it right next to "Jesus Saves": "Mental Illness—The Loneliest Disease."

Lefty responded well to Thorazine, but the political climate was such that Governor Reagan's cost cutting and the liberals' cry to deinstitutionalize conspired to put the mentally ill back on the streets. Lefty moved from a state hospital to a community care facility supported mostly by government funds.

An immigrant family owned the house. The wife had completed the short program to become a licensee of the state, but other than that, they had no formal training. Mrs. Galera had heard from her cousin that this was a good, easy way to make a living in the United States.

The inspector who made periodic visits to Tranquility House had once been passed a note by a crazy named Carl who'd written all in capital letters on plain white paper:

SINCE I HAVE STAYED HERE EVERY LAW FOR THE PROTECTION OF CLIENTS OF BOARD AND CARE HOMES HAS BEEN BROKEN. CHILDREN ARE LIVING ON THE PREMISES. THE MAN AND WIFE THAT OPERATE THE BOARD AND CARE HOME ARE OVERWEIGHT. THE STAFF HAS SERVED KANGAROO MEAT AND BUZZARD MEAT FOR DINNER. THEY HOARD CIGARETTES AND DOLE THEM OUT MANY TIMES A DAY. WE ARE NOT ALLOWED TO HAVE POSSESSION OF OUR MEDS. PEOPLE KEEP STEALING MY CLOTHES. THIS WEEK SOMEBODY TOOK ALL OF MY RINGS AND JEWELRY. THEY SERVED POISONOUS DOG MEAT LAST SUNDAY FOR DINNER.

Tranquility House eventually closed, but not because of any buzzard or dog meat. The Galeras had been cited more than once for many offenses: mouse droppings in the cupboards, understaffing, and failure to meet nutritional standards. But the worst offense was that they let their children sleep in the same rooms as the clients. So perhaps one could say there was an element of truth in the note passed to the inspector.

The Galeras wouldn't give up any of their clients to open space for their children, and room additions would have eaten up their profits, so in stubborn, greedy ignorance, they lost their license, a not uncommon occurrence.

Lefty was released to the custody of his parents. Louise liked only the *idea* of suffering. She liked the drama of the stories about Lefty, and she liked the attention his illness reaped. She loved to make him care packages, to write him letters, to visit him and to pray for him, but, she wasn't, at heart, a martyr, and that's why she and William, Sr. rented the apartment on Lostart Street for Lefty.

No one could have predicted the voice of God would return to command him to take the knife, to walk calmly down to Lostart Street and to sneak behind the apartments. There the smoke of hell greeted him with its stench of burning rubber as he began his descent to kill the devil snuggling against Punky Hayes and to liberate the soul of his fellow lefty.

The Copper Penny Behind the Fuse

Florence remained at the hospital with Mrs. Bean as long as she could. Mrs. Bean's heart attack had been mild, and she would be released soon, unless her insurance coverage was particularly good.

When Florence returned to the apartments, she went immediately to work in the laundry room, drinking past her normal, tipsy state and dwelling on who would take her to the hospital if she had a heart attack. She hoped she was building good karma, that people would feel indebted, that someone would help her, but she doubted it.

At moments like this, her body clenched tight against her son for abandoning her and tighter still against her husband for deserting her. He'd used the suicide as a reason to dump her during his mid-life crisis. She chased her thoughts around and around and around until they made her dizzy, and there was no answer, just an increasing blur. How could a person live a certain life for twenty-odd years—with all the ups and downs of that life—and then have it vanish, as if she were Cinderella and the clock had struck twelve?

She blamed her body for sagging. She blamed her skin for drying and her hair for graying. She accused her husband of wanting a younger, more vibrant woman. She blamed her son for his incurable depression. She blamed him for wearing her clothes to do it. She blamed the world for being too hard for her son to bear. But most of all she blamed herself for a zillion reasons.

In the physical world, perpetual motion may have been impossible, but in her mind, it was not. Drinking was a circuit breaker for the whirring, painful cycle of thoughts, the Catherine's wheel of thoughts.

In truth, the drinking operated much like the copper penny behind one of Mrs. Bean's fuses.

Cowlickcoo—The Calico Cat

If someone had told Cecile she shared a literary interest with Florence, she would have scoffed. Yet, T.S. Eliot, who'd written *The Love Song of J. Alfred Prufrock*, had also written *Old Possum's Book of Practical Cats.* Florence gave a copy of this book to anyone with the slightest fondness for cats at the first special occasion that presented itself. If there weren't any special occasions, she'd create one in order to share this joy. Seeing *Cats*, the Broadway musical based on the book, topped her bucket list.

Florence felt contempt for people who pointed out how many cats she had, as if the cats were all the same. She loved the way T.S. understood the fine distinctions of cat personalities, ranging from that of Jennyanydots to that of Macavity. Even cats as sly and mysterious as Macavity didn't desert you, which made cats a cut above humans.

And here she had abandoned Cowlickcoo, the Calico Cat, to save Mrs. Bean. Cowlickcoo was a neurotic cat with tufts of black, honey-colored and white hair sticking in various directions. She was a veteran chair stealer, but if she couldn't find a properly warm seat, a newly shed pair of socks would do. When traumatized, she peed in the house, and there was no way to predict and avoid the mess, because the oddest things stressed Cowlickcoo. Like a needy person, Cowlickcoo stalked warmth and comfort.

In her stupor, Florence remembered that the poor cat was stuck—alone—in Mrs. Bean's apartment. In the panic of the heart attack and the frantic flagging down of the sheriff, Florence had forgotten Cowlickcoo. Florence started to cry at her own cruelty and planned to jump up and rescue poor Cowlickcoo, but instead, she passed out in the lounger, oblivious to Vince sleeping with Punky and unaware of Lefty Hunt with the butcher knife.

But the sense of smell, the gut level, immediate, underrated sense, sneaked through Florence's alcoholic haze. Black smoke, stinking like tar, alerted her.

Cowlickcoo didn't like the smell of Mrs. Bean's chair and instead had curled half on the windowsill with her rump on the toaster, warm from Mrs. Bean's preparation of an English muffin. She kneaded the sill as if it were a scratching post and yowled at the kitchen window glass. Upset to find herself locked in a strange, crazy place, she had relieved herself, and the pee ran into the old, rusty toaster.

The urine seeped and corroded its way into the electrical system, but the poor, calico cat was not to blame for what happened. Several lights had been left on, drawing electricity, and the penny behind the fuse, to "fix" a short in the electrical system, allowed for a continual current, bypassing the fuse so that it wouldn't constantly blow. This "solution" to the problem guaranteed a fire eventually.

Fire

Lying in bed, I smelled the smoke as it puffed in my open kitchen window, but, even when I got up to investigate, I wasn't convinced of the fire's proximity until I heard its crackle. My trembling fingers searched the pages of the phone book for the fire department's number. Sirens were shrilling from the fire station three blocks away before I thought to simply dial 911.

I pulled on some sweatpants, picked up my school record book and hurried from my apartment to the end of the drive where the first fire truck was arriving. Florence staggered into Lostart Street, gesticulating toward the back for the firemen.

Barefooted and beaming, Vince and Punky stumbled from their love nest. Punky carried Todd wrapped in a blanket, his small feet dangling against her brightly flowered, turquoise kimono. The mother and child pinched their noses at one another and giggled with contagious happiness although, for all they knew, the fire could have been at Vince's. The source of their happiness was buttoning his shirt and combing his sun-bleached hair with his fingers.

The Fat Lady waddled from her apartment dressed, apparently for work, in an ankle length orange muumuu covered with hibiscus. I'd never seen her dressed up before. She wore large hibiscus earrings, red lipstick and red sandals. For a half second, she pulled everyone's attention from the fire, like a blaze of her own. I could see why chubby chasers chased her.

Bucky appeared wearing a full set of flannel pajamas and slippers and hugging a squirming Dudu, sans ribbons, against his chest. A second fire truck stopped at the hydrant on Lostart Street and a third trailed the first one up the drive.

Slurring her words, Florence explained to the fireman-in-command that Mrs. Bean was in the hospital and didn't have to be rescued. The battalion chief sent word to the fire truck at the hydrant to run a hose back.

"Stand back! Stand back!" the battalion chief shouted at us, although even The Fat Lady had joined us at the end of the drive away from the smoke, and we were all pressing toward Punky's place, giving the firemen wide berth to drag the hose past. Three men had come on each engine and all towered above six feet and bulged with muscles. They seemed like a different strain of humanity, powerful and heroic, so in contrast to us, people like—

"The Invisible Lady," I cried.

One of the firemen lugging the hose barely turned to give me the contemptuous look reserved for trouble-making kooks. I could see his sneer in the light from the windows and the blaze, but the people of Lostart Street knew what I meant. We huddled and conferred about whether The Invisible Lady needed to come out.

I finally tugged on the sleeve of the fireman who seemed least vital to the hose and told him the problem.

"I'll check on her." He trotted off.

I moved far enough up the drive to watch him rap on the windows, call out, and finally pound on the door. After an effort that would have stirred the heaviest sleeper, he walked back. "No one's home."

He returned to the fire.

Heroes

The residents stared at one another, so intent on this mystery they didn't notice Lefty's arrival. He had crept through Punky's apartment and finding it vacant, stood now in her doorway, silhouetted by the light, his fingers clenched around the hilt of the butcher knife and his eyes locked on Vince.

"Stay back!" the battalion chief barked in his carnival vibrato, as if he could sense their restlessness. "We don't want a bunch of crispy critters."

The word critter triggered Florence's memory. "Cowlickcoo!" she screamed, raising her arms in the air and fluttering her hands like tattered flags.

The firemen were dousing the building.

"Oh, God, my cat!" Florence wailed, bolting toward the burning apartment. "My cat's in there!"

Lefty lunged at the very moment Vince pounced forward, grabbed Florence's arm, and spun her away from the burning building.

The knife rammed into Florence's belly. Stunned, Florence staggered back, Vince stumbling under her weight.

"You're a tricky bastard," Lefty said. "How did you get behind her?"

Lefty wrenched the knife from Florence's gut. "I'm sorry." He'd run the blade in with a lot of force and it took a moment to extract.

"You're nuts." Florence watched the inches of bloody steel appear from her stomach like some sort of magic trick. She cupped the warm ooze where the first red leaked through her shirt, but she couldn't feel any pain. This is it, she thought. Even as Lefty raised the bloody blade to try again, Florence turned to Vince without a flinch. "You should have let me get Cowlickcoo."

Lefty's arm swayed like a cobra's body, the knife a deadly fang aimed at the distracted Vince.

"Stop it! Stop it!" Bucky shouted at Lefty, his speech impediment vanished, or maybe, Florence thought, she'd stopped hearing it. He let Dudu spring to the ground, and the Hallmark-card ball of fluff growled and took after Lefty's ankle.

"Ahhhhh!" Lefty bleated, dropping the knife to swat Dudu.

Bucky caught the off-balance Lefty by the arm and twirled him to the hard asphalt. "Help me!" Bucky shouted.

The Fat Lady moved first. "I'll sit on the bastard." She plopped on Lefty's chest so hard they all heard his fart-like expulsion of air. Her muumuu ballooned out to cover Lefty's body. She rested her swollen feet on the arms Bucky pinned to the blacktop. As Florence sank toward the ground, Punky rushed to her.

All this happened before the firemen took their attention from the flames, in about the time it took Cecile's frozen scream to thaw.

The Sparks

I kept a palm over my mouth as two firemen bandaged Florence. Was our town so small there were no EMTs? At least the firemen seemed to know what they were doing.

"It looks like you'll be okay," one said.

"You never can tell what's happening inside," the other replied.

"Thanks a lot," Florence mumbled, her face blanched.

"Well, if he got your liver or lungs, you'd be gone by now," the first fireman said, tugging down her shirt over gauze and tape. He put a coat over her. I knew from the disaster preparedness drill at school that Florence was probably in shock.

A third fireman had radioed for an ambulance and a sheriff. Caged between the legs of The Fat Lady and draped in her flowered muumuu from neck to ankles, Lefty seemed completely subdued and disoriented, but a fourth fireman hovered near Bucky and The Fat Lady to make certain the dangerous Lefty didn't pop back into the picture.

Punky bowed over Todd with her back forming a barrier between her child and the violence of the world. Vince placed a protective arm around Punky. My heart yearned for the strength and warmth of an embrace like that.

"Are you all right?"

Strength and warmth circled me. A fireman was wrapping a jacket about my shoulders.

By screaming, I'd broadcast my need to the world. The man crouched so he could peer into my eyes, as if I were a little girl. He had pitted skin, but brown eyes so solicitous they scorched at the casement I'd spent a year and a half constructing around my heart. I felt myself melting to the idea of someone caring for me and looking after me.

I doused these warm gushies with icy water. That type of dependency had caused me nothing but pain, and I'd vowed never to be there again.

"I'm fine," I lied, flapping the jacket back to him as if to beat out any sparks.

A Glimmer of Enlightenment for Vince

Slowly, but logically and inevitably, Vince realized the butcher knife had been intended for him. When The Fat Lady lifted herself from Lefty, the dazed young man offered his wrists for the sheriff's handcuffs, muttering that God had told him to kill the devil. Vince now recalled the shouts outside Punky's door. To Lefty Hunt, *he* was the devil.

The dilatory ambulance carted off Florence with fanfare, its siren wailing and red light whirling. That could have been his body in the vehicle shrieking up Soquel Drive. The firemen picked up their gear. Even though a cat had died in the fire, they had no doubt seen worse. As the men departed, Vince stared wildly at his neighbors. Even in his desperation, he could see they were a motley crew: a fat lady, an English teacher, and a man with limited mental ability. Without Florence they seemed sprung awry like spokes without a hub.

"Do you guys realize he was trying to kill me?" Vince asked. "I was the devil. Remember, Punky? He called me that?"

Punky put her arm around him.

Vince's shoulders sagged. "Jesus, I shouldn't have turned Florence around."

"Shhhh," she said, carrying Todd with one arm and leading Vince with the other hand. "There's no way anyone could have predicted what he was trying to do. He's crazy. Don't blame yourself. If you blame yourself, I have to blame myself. After all, he was after you because of me."

Vince couldn't fault her logic. He followed her into her apartment.

He and the child and Punky all got into bed together, but only the child went to sleep and even he whimpered in the night as though he were having bad dreams.

Vince and Punky lay side-by-side holding hands. Normally he might have gone to the laundry room with his need to vent, but Florence was not there. Florence might not ever be there again. He stared into the darkness. She was just a drunk, and yet he always felt better after he talked to her. For some reason, in spite of the catnapping, she seemed to really like him.

"Do you suppose they took her to Dominican Hospital?" he whispered.

"Probably," Punky murmured, squeezing his hand. "We'll find out and go visit her tomorrow. We can visit Mrs. Bean at the same time."

They lay awake, but sometime in the morning he finally dozed. He awoke to a brilliant Friday morning with the birds singing and the warm, cuddly Punky next to him. He lurched up, terror in his stomach. In the commotion he hadn't set an alarm. When the night had begun centuries ago, he hadn't intended to stay with Punky. He sprang from the bed.

"Vince?" Punky asked. "What's the matter?"

"Some of us are supposed to go to work," he said, instantly regretting his harshness. She had the phone right by her bed, and he dialed his work number. They'd probably tried to call him and hadn't received an answer. At best they were worried about him—he was, after all, very reliable—but, at worst, they'd be pissed.

"Airesearch," the receptionist chirped.

He asked her to put him through to his supervisor.

Instead the receptionist recognized his voice and said, "Vince, are you playing hooky today?"

"Look, Wendy, you wouldn't believe my story if I told you,

so let me talk to my supervisor."

"Are you sure you want to do that?"

"Why?"

"He's not too kindly disposed toward you right now, if you get my drift."

"I have a good story."

"Oh, it's not just that you didn't come in and didn't call or anything. That's the icing on the cake. He was already mad when he left yesterday."

"I left about five minutes before he usually does, Wendy, and he wasn't mad at me when I left. How could he have gotten pissed at me after I was gone?"

"Well, first of all, you forgot to take your bottle of mice with you, and secondly, he could have gotten pissed at you after you were gone because someone told him how that pallet in the basement got broken."

"That's ridiculous! That pallet was already cracked."

"Look, Vince, don't get fired up at me. You know, that's really your problem."

"What's my problem?"

"You have sandpaper in your craw."

Before Vince could reply, he heard the dead sound that meant Wendy was transferring the call.

Bad Luck Can't Last Forever

When Vince's supervisor suspended him from work that day, calling it, on the phone, "a mandatory sick leave," Punky didn't say anything. She secretly congratulated the receptionist and supervisor for doing what Punky now considered her dirty work, to help Vince smooth out his abrasive personality.

Punky viewed relationships as two people rubbing together their rough edges to become better, more polished, human beings. His roughness would buff her to a shine, and, in the meantime, he'd be worn smooth. They did, she insisted to herself, have a relationship, although neither of them could define it, but then, a person never could define a relationship, not if it was healthy and growing.

She commiserated with Vince, but personally was happy about the day's suspension because every time she looked at unit nine she half expected to see Lefty Hunt appear. With Vince nearby, she felt safe.

Vince seemed begrudgingly glad for the day off, too. He sat on the futon. Out loud he mulled over Wendy's comment. He frowned at Punky. "Maybe there's some truth to it?"

Punky stayed quiet and bustled in the tiny kitchen, letting Vince process the feedback.

"Wendy is a sweet gal," he said. "Seriously she is completely impervious to sarcasm. No wit at all. So I think she meant it." He scratched at a finger. "But she's not too bright."

He glanced up at Punky. "And what's wrong, anyway, with speaking the truth?"

His sunny face clouded up. "But deducting the cost of the pallet from my check—that's just not right." He stalked to the phone and protested the unfairness to his boss.

She couldn't hear the boss's side of the conversation, but Punky could see that nothing stirred Vince's heart like injustice. A typical Libra, she thought, but again, wisely, opted not to say anything. Instead she brewed coffee, steeped tea, and toasted bagels for breakfast.

Vince helped Todd put on his shoes. She'd been unfair to Vince with her first judgment. He was not the insensitive, unkind jock she'd imagined. Even if he did refer to Todd as a varmint, his actions belied the words. Or maybe varmint was an affectionate word in Vince's world of mice and snakes and lizards.

Punky put the plate of warm, buttered bagels on the floor by Todd and Vince. The two were now squatted before the terrarium, inspecting Love.

"She looks better," Vince said. "She tried to run when I reached for her. Maybe she was just mourning the loss of Peace."

"You know," Punky said, "I bet Lefty Hunt came in my house and stole Peace." She shivered to verbalize this fear. Unspoken, it had remained nebulous, gossamer, like the feeling of running into an unseen spider's web. Spoken, the old fear hardened—cold and stark—like the knife blade stuck into Florence's belly and pulled out with plums of her blood clinging to the silver.

Punky's mouth collected saliva as if she were going to vomit.

"I wouldn't doubt it," Vince said as he bit into a bagel.

Vince, Mr. Logical himself, was giving credence to her fear. Punky retched but there was absolutely nothing in her stomach.

Vince studied her.

"It's okay. I'm not going to puke."

She castigated herself. If she hadn't dismissed her own intuition, back when Peace disappeared, maybe the truth about Lefty would have been revealed sooner. If she'd called the Sheriff's Department again when the first cruiser vanished, maybe last night would not have happened. She broke Todd's bagel so he couldn't twirl it around his finger anymore.

On the other hand, her impressions of Lefty could have been as erroneous as her impressions of Vince. A person had to cut some slack for people. But with all that had happened, perhaps that wasn't wise. She sighed. If she didn't give the benefit of the doubt, didn't she become jaded, given to forgone conclusions, prejudiced?

She'd bitten meditatively into a bagel when the phone rang in the bedroom. She kept her phone there, a safety precaution learned in The City, not that it had done much good. Someone had entered this apartment—twice—and she hadn't even known.

When Punky returned from the phone, Vince had Todd hoisted before the kitchen sink and was washing his face and fingers. "Do you want to go to Dominican to see what we can find out?" he asked her.

She smiled. The phone call had been good news and after so much bad luck, she wanted to laugh. "That was the Unemployment Office," she said. "They want me to come in today. They have a possible interview for me at a private grocery store that deals in specialty items, gourmet food, that kind of stuff. Very Santa Cruz. They're non-union but they'll pay well for an efficient cashier. They even have some health benefits. The woman at the Unemployment Office said she naturally thought of me. I have all the right qualifications, and she said I was one of the few people she thought wanted a job and wasn't just going through the motions in order to collect a check."

Vince listened, eyes wide.

She could tell the mood change was a little too much for him—fifteen minutes of Punky melancholic sadness, followed by her talking a mile a minute.

Vince lifted Todd in the air and then swung him to the floor in a way that made the child squeal with delight.

"What time do you need to go?" Vince asked.

"The woman at the Unemployment Office wants me to be there at one o'clock."

"What did you tell her?"

"I said I wanted to come today, but I had to arrange a baby-sitter, and I didn't know if I could do that, so I'd call her back."

"Go call her back," Vince said.

She studied his face, tenderness welling up in her.

"Quick," he said. "Before I change my mind."

"God, you're great." She threw her arms around him. More than the sex (which had been good) and more than the security his presence gave her, the voluntary help flooded her with love for him. "I'll pay you," she whispered in his ear.

"You don't have that kind of money," he grumped. "But we could take it out in trade."

The Lesson

My proclivity toward organization unraveled. I couldn't teach the stuff penciled neatly, in detail, under Friday, November 4, in my lesson book. If I hadn't already missed Monday, I would have called for a substitute.

Instead, as first bell rang, I sat on the ledge of my lectern, butterflies in my stomach at the imminent prospect of "winging it." My freshmen entered, not at all like the squirrelly monsters in the horror stories I'd heard before I'd started my job.

Warm-hearted and big-footed, they stumbled in, not yet hyped with the bravado they manufactured or marked with the cowering they manifested to avoid being stuffed into garbage cans. Just one of the terrifying things they'd heard upper classmen would do.

They'd only begun to ingest their candy and colas. For now, they were as vulnerable as babies awakened from naps.

Rosaura had been absent since Tuesday. Earlier, I'd dropped by her counselor's office.

"Her family is migrant," the woman pronounced matter-of-factly. "They follow the crops. They've probably moved on to Arizona."

No wonder Rosaura had wished to be a mountain, fixed in place. Disappointment must have shown on my face because the counselor chirped. "They'll be back in the spring."

"I wish she'd said goodbye." Then I realized she had. The

churro had been a goodbye present.

As the second bell rang, the students settled into their desks, but the room felt empty. One missing person and the whole atmosphere changed.

The students quieted, looked at me, waited. I'd done a great job of training them in only two months.

I shot a quick glance at Annette, bent over her papers at her desk. "I don't think I'll teach today," I said.

Ruben clapped. A few giggled and commented. Then they returned to an even more receptive attention, expecting me to teach.

"I had a lesson prepared, but I can't teach it." I could feel Annette's eyes boring into me. Was I about to unleash chaos in her room?

Ruben slouched in his seat and crossed his ankles. His back-to-school haircut was now a two-inch bush. "Are we going to kick back?"

"Why can't you teach your lesson?" Liliana asked. "What happened to it?"

"Yeah," Ruben chimed. "Did your dog eat it?"

"Well, last night there was a fire and a stabbing where I live."

Ruben pulled himself up straight in his desk. "Where do you live? Across the bridge?"

The class erupted into questions. Again, in my short teaching career, I had every student engaged. The stories of apathy simply weren't true. When something seemed immediate and important, their interest soared, but to seem important the topic needed a touch of the personal, of the human. The period ended with them still asking questions, some that I couldn't answer like, "Where will Mrs. Bean live?"

As I passed by Annette's desk, she said, "Pretty interesting." And then to my surprise, muttered, "Glad you're okay."

That day would have been chaos if I had not already established an atmosphere of discipline and respect. But, I thought, there had to be a way to hitch an agenda to all that curiosity.

The Invisible Lady's note resonated in my head: *help your students to be human.* I'd learned that I could help them to be human by sharing myself, a good person, an adult, a role model, and not by effacing myself behind the lesson plan on the board. If I wanted them to show interest in the lessons, my class had to be real life because that was where their interest thrived. I had to work more, not less, on my lesson plans to find the connections.

I went home that day certain that I learned more from my students than they learned from me.

The Invisible Lady Appears

Telling my students for five periods about the fire and the stabbing objectified the events until they seemed like something I'd seen on television. When the students asked their questions, I realized I'd missed so many details, I doubted the reality.

Exhausted, I drove up the asphalt drive, scouting for clues of what had transpired the night before. An aura of stillness surrounded the front units, although Vince's Datsun was parked in the driveway. Toward the back, the charred remains of Mrs. Bean's apartment, encircled with caution tape, looked about to collapse.

A huge box emerged from Florence's apartment walking on a pair of tiny, unmistakable legs propped in two-inch red heels. Bobbi Headland leaned backward as she carried the load toward the dumpster.

Even though my students' questions buzzed in my head, Bobbi Headland was not the person I wanted to answer them. And now did not seem like the appropriate time to complain about the roaches. I had a sudden ache for Florence to be in the laundry room. I delayed getting out of my Volkswagen while Bobbi trudged by with the box. What was she doing in Florence's apartment anyway?

I climbed from my bug with my usual cargo—book bag, purse, lunch sack, and bundle of keys. The apartment complex smelled of old damp smoke. I could bear smokers puffing live cigarettes and fires pluming smoke on the beach, but ashtrays and dead fires stank of death and disappointment. The reek reminded me of the persistent, sulfur stench choking my hometown, a smell that wrapped my classmates who stayed and married and had babies.

Soot smeared the front of my ugly, mustard-colored apartment, but I was lucky to have a place to live. I opened the door without getting my mail so I could be inside before Bobbi Headland returned. I sat at my desk by the window to spy on her.

"You fucking cunt!"

The Invisible Lady's words hurled into the driveway and shattered all my illusions of her.

Bobbi Headland halted right in front of my window and pivoted toward The Invisible Lady's unit. "You should know a thing or two before you start screaming obscenities," Bobbi said.

"What do I need to know to recognize a bitch raiding my friend's house?" The Invisible Lady shouted.

For the first time, I could hear her. This was not the private, celebratory language of an Emily Dickinson recluse.

"Florence died last night in the ambulance," Bobbi shot back.

I gasped, but The Invisible Lady did not miss a beat. The door to her apartment flew open and a wheelchair sprang from the landing to the blacktop. I gasped again at the sight of the legless woman in the chair with auburn tresses streaming behind her like a battle flag. I sprang to my feet.

"That's   fucking   convenient,   isn't   it?"   the No-Longer-Invisible Lady yelled at Bobbi as she charged with the wheelchair. Strong arms madly pushed the wheels. This apparition apparently didn't believe Bobbi, but then, she had not seen the stabbing, had not witnessed the length of steel wrenched from Florence's belly. I felt sick to my core, a little wobbly on my legs.

Bobbi Headland dodged the chair, but the woman popped a wheelie, turned, and propelled her legless body and her chair toward the tiny apartment manager in her red pumps.

Bobbi jumped aside again, and again the woman popped the wheelchair around as though the absence of legs made it airy. She aimed her vehicle at the frightened redhead panting in the middle of the driveway and tipping from her red perches.

First Lefty and now this one. It was too much, but at least this time I didn't freeze. I heard The Visible Lady's next words from my step.

"You've been looking for a chance to get rid of Florence," The Visible Lady shouted, her face contorted with wrath. "You're just too much of a chicken shit to come when she's here."

"I tell you Florence is dead," Bobbi screamed. "It was internal hemorrhaging."

If The Visible Lady made another charge at Bobbi, I planned to grab the back of her chair, but the specific words, *internal hemorrhaging,* deflated her. The broad shoulders sagged, the muscled torso collapsed, and the thick, wavy hair dropped forward over defeated breasts.

"Don't you think I care?" Bobbi said, sensing her advantage.

The manager glanced toward me conspiratorially.

My stomach turned. I disliked her. Intensely.

The Visible Lady raised her head. "Frankly, I don't think you give a shit about anybody."

"Well, just so you know," Bobbi huffed, her offended glance including me as if she knew my sympathy had shifted, "I'm clearing Florence's apartment so Mrs. Bean will have a place to live."

"How very altruistic of you," The Visible Lady said as she whizzed past Bobbi to her apartment.

I ran down my steps, thinking to assist The Visible Lady, to let her know I was on her side. In her chair, she had flown from the single step that now, to me, seemed insurmountable.

"What do you want?" The Visible Lady snapped at me. I felt Bobbi Headland smirking as her red heels snick-snacked toward Florence's; I would have been offended at the Visible

Lady's tone if I hadn't seen the telltale shimmer of tears in her eyes.

"Hold open the door," the woman said.

I did as commanded. The Visible Lady tipped her wheelchair to a rakish angle, skipped over the single step, turned on the landing, and pushed through the open door.

"Thank you," she said curtly, in dismissal.

The Roller Coaster of Life

Punky got the job at the family-run grocery store, and Vince took Todd with him to Dominican where he learned of Florence's death. The two met later at Punky's apartment, Vince long-faced and full of sorrow and Punky glittering and full of joy. Punky resented the undermining of her elation. It had been a long time since she'd felt as good as she had at the store when the manager, a woman, asked, "When can you start?"

The hardwood floors of the store gleamed. The workers moved at a slow, gracious pace and items were displayed to look irresistible. Although a bit yuppie for her, the store certainly was a hell of a lot more personal than Lucky's, and the manager seemed warm and honest.

She had the job. All she had to do was line up childcare. Lefty Hunt was out of her life, and Vince, for now, was in it, so when he met her at the door with his bubble-popping news of Florence's death, she simply could not bear it. She burst into unabashed tears.

The pitches of her emotions no longer mystified Vince, but he still held her ineffectually. Florence's death left him hollow and sharply aware of his mortality, but not sad or tearful. He'd longed for the reassurance of Punky's company, and instead had received a weeping woman. He couldn't know she cried bitterly for a lost happiness, for a sad knot of complication in her stomach that threatened she might never experience an unqualified emotion again.

Their awkward embrace came apart when they heard yelling. All three of them went out the door to witness The Visible Lady in her wheelchair chasing Bobbi Headland as the English teacher gawked at the scene from her steps.

"She doesn't drive that thing like an old maid," Vince commented, not caring a dot, not even a molecule, if The Visible Lady rammed into Bobbi Headland.

Punky sniffled. Her nose twitched, and she laughed, heartily, throwing back her head, the thick hair reaching her butt. She didn't really believe, after all, that a woman in a wheelchair would hurt anyone.

"You notice the weirdest things, Vince," she choked through her laughter, strangling on the words.

Vince stared at her. Her moods swung as wildly as the woman in the wheelchair.

Vince didn't realize, as Punky did, how close tears and laughter resided. The wheelchair, hopping over the step, punctuated the end of the scene.

Oh, For a Heart With Wings

I wanted Florence in the laundry room to console me for her own death. What happened to her remains if no relative showed up? To have no one at your death seemed like the most lost and alone a person could be. At least I had family, even if they were as far across the country as was geographically possible, and even further away culturally.

Homework papers heaped before me on my desk. What would happen if I "lost" them, if I took them to the beach and let the breeze liberate them, lift them into the sky like white doves. They could fly off like Florence's spirit. What would it matter in the end?

Instead of attacking the work before me, I fantasized about the ugly fireman with the gorgeous eyes. I crossed my legs and swung them vigorously and considered calling Imogene in The City, but on Friday night she'd be watching an old flick at the Roxy, catching the plays at One Act Theater, or having coffee and a treat at Just Desserts or, at least, that's where I'd be if I had a hot new love to accompany me.

I picked up the top essay and sighed. That was my old life. My former life. I needed to carve out that kind of life here. Find havens, sanctuaries . . . people . . . friends.

Perhaps I should put an ad in the *Good Times*: *Twenty-eight-year-old, thin, nice-looking English teacher desires to meet SWM, disease free, for coffee, movies, dinners, beach walks, literary discussions, sex.*

Terribly uncreative, I thought. I wouldn't answer it.
Scarred heart would like to have wings again.

Mr. PROPRTY

Saturday unfolded. The stench of the damp, charred wood assaulted me as I sat on my step. The structure next door retained its shape although mostly blackened and gutted inside. The firemen had warned us to stay away from it.

Sun spilled over the asphalt and glared off the papers on my lap. A cool sea breeze riffled them occasionally so I had to keep one hand on them when I paused to sip my coffee or to glance surreptitiously at The Invisible Lady's window.

Down past the laundry room, Vince, Punky and Todd sat like Papa Bear, Mama Bear and Baby Bear on Punky's steps. The setting filled me with déjà vu, not for an event, but for a feeling. Once upon a time the apartment complex had seemed peaceful, like this.

I broke the spell by waving. They all waved back—Punky with an exaggerated arc, Todd with a childish flapping of the hand, Vince with a salute.

About midday Bobbi Headland showed up again, wearing skintight Guess jeans, canary yellow oversized blouse with turned up collar, canary yellow plastic hoop earrings and plastic beads, and canary yellow pumps, apparently her cleaning outfit since she parked a black plastic garbage bag on either side of Florence's steps.

She glanced toward The Invisible Lady's apartment. I remained seated on my step and watched, but nothing eventful happened. Bobbi disappeared into the apartment.

About one o'clock a metallic blue Cadillac Seville sporting PROPRTY plates rolled supremely over the asphalt and stopped, blocking the driveway, in front of the burned remains of Mrs. Bean's. A man disembarked. Long legs in gray slacks. His silver hair, cut short, had enough length left on top to fall in a debauched fashion across his well-tanned forehead. He had Southern California written all over him.

Standing before Mrs. Bean's, he stretched, a light gray, short-sleeved embroidered shirt falling into place. The gape of his arms was not just that of a man tired from a long drive, but also proprietary, embracing his kingdom, right at home even though a stranger. He inspected the scorched building and loudly clucked his tongue.

"Hello there," he said to me.

"I don't think you can rent it," I said dryly. I had a profound distaste for slumlords.

"Ah, these places don't make me any profit," he retorted with airy nastiness. He'd not missed an iota of my intent and studied me now with hard eyes. "I'd be better off if they all burned."

Rage bubbled in me. These places, my home, had been subjected to a mentally ill person, a fire and a murder, and here he was discussing profits. He probably considered Florence's death a convenient eviction. Rolling up the papers in my lap, I lurched upright. "Three-hundred and twenty-five dollars may seem like peanuts to you, but it's a quarter of my salary for a place with roaches, a stove that leaks gas, constant theft, and an unavailable manager."

Well, I'd spilled that. No measured teaspoon this time.

He marched the short distance to me with his hand thrust out. For once I was glad to see Bobbi Headland coming my way. The hand's impulse must surely have been to hit me, but instead it brusquely shook my hand, which had somehow extended itself. Looking into the man's face, I realized his hair had prematurely silvered and he was quite handsome.

"Citrino," he said gruffly. "John Citrino."

"The owner."

"You got it." He turned toward Bobbi and curled an arm around the skinny woman's shoulder. "Hi ya, Babe." He hugged her sideways, and kissed her forehead. "You're looking good."

I sat back down on my step, very aware that the concrete under my butt didn't belong to me.

"Seems we have a dissatisfied customer," the man said snidely to Bobbi.

"Well, you know how it is, John, with all these crazy things happening here. I haven't had time to deal with normal problems." Bobbi Headland turned to me. "Look, dear," she said in a saccharine voice, "you can call PG&E on that leak. I doubt they'll charge you, and if they do, deduct it from next month's rent."

"Speaking of rents," Citrino switched back to his gruff voice, "this lady said hers is three-twenty-five."

The spiky-lashed eyes with their constant look of surprise widened with genuine alarm. Bobbi Headland looped her arm around the man's. "We need to sit down and chat," she said softly. "In private."

She shot me a glare, laden with hatred, unjustifiably intense for simply going over her head with a complaint. "This has been a hell of a week, John." She stroked the tan biceps.

I sat numbly, certain there would be no next month's rent from which to deduct anything.

Across from me, the door banged open. A flying wheelchair whopped against the blacktop. John Citrino and Bobbi Headland whirled, and Bobbi immediately cowered behind John's back.

"What the fuck?" he said, more shocked it seemed by Bobbi's clutching at the back of his shirt than by The Visible Lady's dramatic entrance.

"What a gutless wimp you have for a manager, John," The Visible Lady chuckled.

John Citrino bristled at the comment. No wonder. The way Bobbi Headland had stroked his arm indicated she served as a bit more than a manager. John Citrino locked his jaw as if to restrain a rebuttal attacking this legless wonder.

"John," The Visible Lady said, "you might like to know I also pay three-twen—"

Bobbi popped from behind the man. "Shut up."

"Three twenty-five," The Visible Lady shouted, shooting backward as Bobbi charged, body lowered and hands extended to push over the chair.

"Shut up, you stupid, fucking cripple!" Bobbi shrieked, tears streaming. She hit with all her fragile might where The Visible Lady's knees would have been if she'd had any. With a quick backward movement of her chair, The Visible Lady pitched Bobbi onto all fours against the asphalt.

John Citrino and I each grabbed an arm and helped her up. She lifted as though every bone were broken although the damage seemed minor, one rip in the forty-dollar jeans, shredded palms, tears smearing the face with mascara, and snot running from her nose.

"Let go of me, bitch," she snarled at me.

I let go, but John Citrino did not. He gripped the thin, freckled arm so it pinched white around his fingers. He plucked a clean, pressed handkerchief from his back pocket and stuck it in Bobbi's free hand. "Clean yourself, Babe. Then we better have that private chat."

As Bobbi mopped her face and blew her reddened nose, The Visible Lady fearlessly wheeled closer. "John, I know I don't have any legs to wrap around your neck, but then I don't have a nose that will snort up your profits, either, and I think I'd make a helluva manager. You can see my handicap doesn't keep me from doing what I need to do."

Citrino glowered at The Visible Lady. He tugged Bobbi toward the Seville, opened the door like a gent, and then pushed her inside. He climbed in the car himself. He did not race the engine or gun it. Bobbi made no attempt to escape. The Visible Lady and I moved out of the way as John Citrino drove majestically away.

For all I could tell, they'd go off and make up and things would revert to normal, except that now the manager would hate our guts and make life miserable for us.

Bobbi kept her head tucked down. The Visible Lady waved at the departing couple.

Something Rotten in the State of Denmark

The Visible Lady tilted her head back like a wolf baying at the moon and laughed.

I drummed my thigh with rolled-up essays. "I don't see what's so funny."

It took a moment for her to contain the laughter. "I'm soooo happy." She hugged her own torso. "I hate that bitch."

"I don't see where we've accomplished anything." I sat on her landing so we'd be more nearly eye-to-eye. Her face was strikingly beautiful, flawless skin and large violet eyes framed with lush auburn hair.

"Well I hope he doesn't murder her." She clapped gleefully. "I believe in cleaning up the environment, but stop short of killing."

"Murder her?" I scoffed. "They looked like they were off to a love shack."

She shook her head. "I've only met John Citrino one time before, but I can tell you there's one thing he values more than pussy."

Money, I gathered.

"You don't get it, do you?"

I shook my head and made a mental note never to use that condescending tone with my students.

"Three twenty-five is not supposed to be our rent. Bobbi's been skimming. I always wondered how she supported her habit."

"Cocaine?" Bobbi's hyped-up manner made sense now.

"By far Alice's biggest customer," The Visible Lady added, matter-of-factly. "But when the police raided Alice's, heh, Bobbi couldn't wait to rent it. I never did like the bitch, but that's when I started to hate her. I wouldn't doubt if she turned in Alice herself in order to turn over the unit and jack up the rent."

The Visible Lady backed up to align her wheelchair with her step and landing.

"Wait a minute." I didn't get up so she'd have to wait—or run over me. I was not at all convinced she wouldn't do the latter. "Could I ask you a couple of questions?"

"That's one," she said snottily.

I sprang up from the concrete landing. To hell with her. I'd die of curiosity. I received enough abuse at school.

"I'm sorry," she said. "I just get so fucking tired of people asking how I lost my legs. Even when they don't ask, they ask. They ask with their exaggerated politeness, or their curious eyes, or with their embarrassment. I'd rather be invisible."

"Then where were you the other night," I blurted, "during the fire?"

She laughed. "I was dancing at the Catalyst."

I'm sure my face revealed all my disbelief. I'd always been a lousy liar, a no talent at poker faces.

"Come on," she said. "Why couldn't I be out dancing?"

Legless? Did she dance on her stumps? Dance in her chair? Was she kidding me?

"Ask Chuck if you don't believe me."

Chuck? I didn't even say it, but she saw the question written all over my face.

"My boyfriend, silly. You've seen him a bunch of times. He comes over every weekend."

Stunned, I stared at this legless beauty wondering whether to take her seriously and what she had looked like when she had legs, if she'd ever had legs.

"Now that's a couple of questions," she said, suddenly curt, but with a hint of a smile.

The Narrator

A quarter cup of half and half diluted my coffee to a proper caramel color. As I sipped reflectively, I thought not of the manager Bobbi Headland or the owner John Citrino or of Florence's upcoming cremation, but of my favorite subject—me. I was an idiot.

Why was I shocked at the idea The Visible Lady might have a boyfriend? Shocked, shit, I hadn't believed it. I'd seen people visit her all the time, why shouldn't one of them be a lover? Well, at first I'd assumed she was old. But, even if she were old, why make those assumptions? Why shouldn't she have a man? But how did they have sex?

Images of various possible positions flashed by. *Stop that. Not nice.*

Why did my mind convert her visitors into relatives? Did I think only people inextricably linked by blood would bother with the old or maimed?

Maybe, because that's the way I was. Well there I went, supposing everyone possessed my faults.

Faults? What did I expect of myself? I was working sixty hours a week and was as nice to these wacky neighbors as I knew how to be. I was too hard on myself. No wonder I was too hard on everyone else. No wonder I didn't believe a woman in a wheelchair might go out and boogie when I, with all my appendages, didn't give myself that kind of break.

I blamed myself for my pregnancy. I blamed myself for having an abortion. I blamed myself for not having the guts to keep the baby. If I could find a way to climb out of this pit, to forgive myself, then maybe I could forgive Angelo, and if I could forgive him, maybe my anger at the world would sink into hell, where it belonged.

Backstory or Legstory

About five o'clock I wandered to The Invisible Lady's window. I squinted into the dimness of her apartment.

"I'm here, Cecile," she said. "Brace yourself. Citrino hasn't shown up, so I'll tell you where I left my legs. I know you're wondering."

I didn't say anything. This woman wielded her handicap like a bludgeon.

"Have you heard of The Highway of Terror out of Quangtri?"

"Vietnam?" I guessed.

"My legs are splattered there."

"You're a Vietnam Vet?"

"Women were there," she stated from the shadows. "I was a nurse. I never considered myself pro-war. That's one of the biggest misconceptions people have about us vets. They seem to think everyone who didn't duck what he'd been taught was his duty was some sort of blood-thirsty brute."

"I don't think that."

"Did I say *you?*"

Wow, she was prickly, or maybe the prickliness only went with the topic she'd chosen.

"You know," she said, "the things people do and say don't have much to do with you, but everything to do with them."

Right-o.

"In my hometown—Colorado Springs—there's a mountain, Cheyenne Mountain, that's hollow and inside is the North American Air Defense Command. My dad was a barber with special clearance to go into that mountain to cut the workers' hair."

My eyes were adjusting and The Visible Lady's words pulled my attention to the beautiful locks flowing around her shoulders.

"He—my dad--learned to shave heads in the army. So I grew up in a pro-military environment."

I didn't say anything. This was clearly a sensitive subject.

"Anyway, I went to nurses' training in Denver and between my studies I watched the results of the Tet Offensive and of Hamburger Hill. I wanted to do something. I felt so impotent watching all that on TV.

"To me all those war protestors were slaps in the faces to the soldiers. The soldiers didn't create the war. Many didn't volunteer to go. They were asked to go, and they were blown to bits. They came from blue-collar families like mine. Those demonstrators were another breed, privileged draft-dodging college kids."

Up through the window her hair swayed back and forth as she shook her head. "But I really did want to go. I dreamed of becoming another Florence Nightingale. I actually feared the war would end before I had a chance to be a heroine. Kissinger was already negotiating with the North Vietnamese. Even after I found out my assignment was in Quangtri near the DMZ, I wasn't scared."

That seemed right. Even now The Visible Lady struck me as a fearless warrior.

She paused. The silence stretched. A mockingbird peeped, trilled, tweeted and peeped again. A muscle car rumbled down Lostart Street.

"So what happened?"

"I got there." She sighed wearily. "No twenty-three-year-old could imagine the reality. When the first casualties were brought in, I thought I'd run. Amputees bothered me most. I remember one boy—he really was a boy, baby-faced, still had acne—his name was Cliff Morgan. He had a bilateral amputation above the knees. I was making rounds and he said, 'Lorraine, how do I write and tell my mother I don't have legs anymore?' I almost cried. Then I thought, 'Wait. I can't cry. I'm the nurse. I'm supposed to comfort him.'"

Outside the window, looking into this hazy past, I realized the rift six or eight years made between us. A typical high-school student, I'd been much more interested in styles and boys than the war on television.

Lorraine. I toyed with the name, trying to plug it and this background into the person of The Invisible Lady. She'd probably never imagined I thought of her as that, since she'd known my name, it seemed, from the beginning. But weren't we all, like fictional characters, realized differently in each person's head?

"I lived in a stunned state," Lorraine croaked. "Lost my appetite for heroics."

I waited. There was nothing to say, no comfort to offer for this sad history.

"When the North Vietnamese attacked on Easter weekend," she continued, "I ran like everyone else. Our truck was piled so high with supplies and workers and wounded that I had to ride with my legs hanging out. So many running people clogged the road that we could barely move. The vehicles looked like grotesque floats decorated with crates of chickens and bicycles. I felt more impotent than I had watching the war on TV. I was there and people were falling and I couldn't do anything.

"Then this whirring came right at me. I couldn't move. The rocket cut through both my legs. If I'd fallen out, I don't know what would have happened. Instead I fell backward into a truck full of medical workers and medical supplies. So I survived. I became a bilateral above-the-knee amputee—just like Cliff."

The cathartic rush of Lorraine's story sounded as if she hadn't told it enough times. Maybe with a story like that, one could never tell it enough times. "You don't sound bitter," I said.

A strangling sound emanated from the window. "Don't let me fool you. I'm very bitter."

"I would be."

"Bitterness is the worst part. I had a great doctor, though. He kept saying, 'Lorraine, the injury won't kill you, but bitterness might.'"

My Big Saturday Night

Oddly, all these events increased my loneliness, as though I'd ventured into the world only to discover I didn't belong in it. By Saturday night, all my papers and lesson plans were done, so I rocked, thinking I should get up and go somewhere. Maybe to a club where there'd be other people. Up the hill from where I lived, probably not even a mile away, was a place called O.T. Price's, with live music.

I went to my closet and inspected my clothes. November evenings could be quite chilly, but I didn't want to wear wool. It'd be too hot if someone asked me to dance. I didn't want to wear layers because I'd have no one with whom to stash any shed clothing. If I chose silk, I'd have to dry clean it after one short wear because of the smoke.

Ah fuck. If you're going out, go out.

You can afford dry cleaning, I told myself. You're a grown woman with a real job.

I unwrapped my silk shift from its plastic shroud. Although the cut was conservative, the pattern seemed daring to me, all black on one side, black and white striped on the other side, with red piping and belt.

I shaved my legs and underarms and showered. Bent over, I blow-dried my hair so it would have body. I filed my fingernails and painted them red. I put on as much make up as I ever wore—mascara, blush and lipstick. I smeared myself with lotion and dabbed perfume behind my ears and knees.

When I'd dressed, I checked myself in a newly acquired full-length mirror. I had a pretty face and a svelte body, but I already felt tired. It was 9:30.

The parking lot beside O.T. Price's was almost full and I had to park deep in the back. I climbed out into a pitch-black maze of cars, a perfect place for a rape or robbery. Which reminded me that we'd never solved the thefts at Lostart Street, although they seemed to have stopped. Maybe the thief had been Lefty Hunt.

I wrapped my arms around myself, my heart thudding under my right wrist. I waited for my eyes to adjust and then shuffled over the gravel in my pumps. Two silhouettes stirred in the backseat of a yellow Charger. I jumped. They turned toward me. I hurried on, thinking how cramped they must be.

Music pulsated through the corrugated-metal wall of the building. Vibrations came up through the concrete front walk. I threw open the door and made my grand entrance.

Straight ahead through the smoke, the lead singer gyrated in a black leather mini skirt, a black leather jacket and a studded belt slung low on narrow hips. Under the jacket, a minuscule black top bared her midriff and exposed most of her cleavage. Long raven hair snarled and twisted over her shoulders. She was not singing now, but dancing to a complicated guitar riff. She turned her back to the audience and twitched her butt, which brought a round of applause.

My enthusiasm drained. I felt old, and when I looked around, I felt even older. The crowd went for black, preferably leather, and peroxided hair. One needed at least seven or eight earrings to fit in and Doc Martens or high tops. Some of the students at Watsonville dressed like this, and for a moment I panicked, thinking one of them might be here with a fake I.D., and see me in the entrance.

The man at the door let me stand, undisturbed by more

than an occasional sidelong glance. He was older than the crowd and dressed in Levi's and a sweatshirt, a man from my generation, the tail-end of the boomers.

The small dance floor remained empty, even though all the tables seemed full, and people teemed around the bar to my right. The sweet cloying odor of clove cigarettes drifted toward me.

A couple, probably the ones I'd disturbed in the parking lot, came in behind me. I stepped aside, and when they moved ahead of me to pay their admissions, I slipped out the door.

Mrs. Bean's Return

Mrs. Bean came home on Sunday. The yellow cab rolled up the driveway through the fog as I sat at my desk drinking coffee. The car stopped by the burned structure.

The driver twisted around. "This is it?" he said, loudly as though he thought Mrs. Bean were deaf, too.

I couldn't hear if she replied. I waited several minutes for her to pay him. The day was quiet, as Sunday mornings were, especially when fog muffled the distant noise of the freeway.

I moved to the steps, thinking Mrs. Bean might extract herself from the cab, realize she had no home to return to, and die of another heart attack on the spot.

As Mrs. Bean finally did swivel her legs out the back door and lift herself unsteadily on to her cane, the neighborhood converged on her as though everyone shared my thoughts.

Lorraine rolled her wheelchair to her landing, Punky and Vince, both in robes, leaned out Punky's door, and through the haze, Bucky and Dudu galloped down the asphalt, a scarlet ribbon bouncing on Dudu's white fur. The Fat Lady waddled down her steps and then stood impassive as a lighthouse.

Mrs. Bean seemed oblivious to us, but the driver didn't. His head swung this way and that on its hammy neck, stunned by the sudden life, the apparitions in the gloom. As soon as Mrs. Bean hobbled safely around the back of the car, he tore off, burning rubber.

Squarely before her home, Mrs. Bean stopped. Her head moved in a slow circle as her old eyes took in the sight. She raised her hand to her heart, and her cane clattered to the ground.

Bucky and Dudu reached her first. Lorraine flew from her landing as I ran down from mine.

Whatever momentary pain she might have felt, Mrs. Bean apparently had no intention of having another heart attack.

She swiped at us with both scrawny arms.

"Good Golly!" she said disgustedly as she flailed at us. "What do you all want?"

One of her bony arms clobbered Bucky on the forearm and when he yelped, Dudu pounced at the disoriented old lady, yapping and nipping.

"Get that horrid little cat killer out of here," Mrs. Bean shouted. "This is private property."

Bucky collared the dog and backed away from the ungrateful old sourpuss. A racist, too, I reminded myself.

"If he bites me, I'll sue," she screeched after the figure retreating into the fog.

Mrs. Bean bent as if to retrieve her cane, but Lorraine rolled over, snatched it up, and handed it to the woman. I doubted the wisdom of supplying Mrs. Bean with a blunt instrument, but Lorraine didn't flinch as she sat blocking the old woman's entrance to the burned building.

"Well, what are you two up to?" Mrs. Bean asked. "I don't plan to go back to that damn hospital, thank you very much," she snapped.

"Mrs. Bean." I stepped over to Lorraine's wheelchair. "We have no intention of making you go back to the hospital, but you can't go in there."

"I know too much about hospitals for my own good," Mrs. Bean muttered.

I half expected her to raise the cane and whack me from her path, but she didn't move. Only her gaze wandered past Lorraine, up the steps, to the door.

"The fire destroyed your home. The inside is gutted. The structure is unsafe." I mouthed the fireman's words, but for some reason making this stand exhilarated me. Lorraine reached over and grasped my hand as a show of unity. Energy shot up my arm to my heart. "If there's anything of value left inside, the firemen should remove it for you."

Mrs. Bean remained very quiet, digesting all this. Finally she spoke, all her persnickety nature gone, her voice reduced to a helpless peep. "Where am I going to live?"

"I have an idea," Lorraine said brightly.

Breaking and Entering

Breaking into Florence's apartment stirred my blood. The tough tomcat posed in the back window, but I hissed at him and he sprang into the weeds. Bobbi had left the window open, probably for the cats. It wasn't even screened, so I grabbed the sill, jumped to get my torso over it, and hoisted myself while my toes pushed furiously against the stucco. Involvement and concentration filled me; no room remained for small anxieties and nagging worries. I'd been hungry for this feeling of complete immersion since the day I'd locked away my writing.

As I wiggled over the sill, I stared right into a carpet decorated with smelly squiggles. I had been about to enter hands first, but changed my mind and scooted around in the small opening, scraping my elbows and pelvic bone, until I straddled the sill.

I extended the first foot, deciding finally to place it in the litter box under the window since the cats obviously were not using it.

The apartment reeked from the droppings, but otherwise Bobbi had done more than I'd imagined. Items of value had been packed in boxes pushed against the wall by the entrance, and full Hefty garbage bags waited in the kitchenette for Bobbi's return after her *chat* with John Citrino. Below the sink, ants attacked a large pan of dry cat food. An old green plastic bowl put down for water looked nearly empty.

I unlocked the front door where Lorraine and Mrs. Bean waited.

"Open the door wide and back away," Lorraine commanded.

The wheelchair apparently gave her the power to boss people around. She took a run at the one shallow step, tilted back into a wheelie, threw her weight forward, and popped up, rolling across the landing.

I had to help Mrs. Bean. There was no rail and she needed my shoulder for leverage. The seconds ticked away as Mrs. Bean wobbled and strained. I worried that John Citrino would return and catch us. Finally Mrs. Bean shuffled across the threshold.

"It's perfect," Lorraine exclaimed. She fairly glowed as she turned her wheelchair this way and that in the space between Florence's rattan chairs. "It's furnished," she said with a sweeping gesture. "It even has cats," she bubbled.

Mrs. Bean's filmy eyes inspected the dubious surroundings, the dirty walls and long strips of peeling paint that Bobbi hadn't been able to do much about yet. Her wrinkled nose wrinkled even more as she sniffed the atmosphere like a bloodhound. "My, Lord, I'll say there are cats."

"I'm sure they're housebroken," I said. "They're just indignant about Florence's absence." Only Cowlickcoo hadn't been fully trained, but I thought better of touching that subject.

"As soon as I'm manager," Lorraine said confidently, "we'll get a rail for the step. Then I'll have the wiring checked and we'll paint the place."

My brows lifted so high they must have hit my hairline. Here we were breaking and entering, and Lorraine had no qualms. She went about redecorating the place in her mind, plunging naively and positively onward, as though she owned the building.

Envy lumped in my throat. Where had Lorraine found this courage—this power? If I were her, I would curse my fate when people sprinted by my chair or pumped by on their bicycles, or merely sat, swinging bare, shapely legs for the world to admire.

But, here I was feeling envious of *her*, of a legless woman in a wheelchair who burned with dreams.

"I want a pink bathroom," Mrs. Bean said.

The Resolution for Punky, Vince and Todd

Vince kissed the sleeping Punky. She was out like a rock—a very soft rock. Since she was so exhausted from the events of the last few weeks, he reset the alarm to ensure she would wake up. Then he gazed at the kid, sleeping at a diagonal halfway down the mattress. Todd's feet had prodded Vince all night. He'd have to talk to Punky about a separate bed for the varmint.

Today, Vince resolved as he climbed into his Datsun, he would confront Pasty Face about the deduction from his check. While he drove "over the hill," as locals called the commute, he ran a dozen versions of the scenario but they all ended with the supervisor blowing up, an inevitability with such an anal-retentive type. Pasty Face didn't like people and had no business supervising, but he impressed the plants' administrators with copious and precise paperwork.

Vince flicked on the radio and heard *Tainted Love*. He patted the steering wheel and sang; he was strictly a car and shower singer.

Next the disc jockey selected a piece constructed specifically for break dancers. Vince had seen Bucky and Dudu with neighborhood boys breakdancing on crushed cardboard in the middle of Lostart Street. Bucky was training the dog to roll on its back and kick its legs in the air, which was funny even if it was a pain in the ass to have the kids blocking the road.

Vince enjoyed watching the kids spin on their backs or

heads. They arched into bridges, hopped upright, and flipped themselves into handstands. Break dancing seemed an appropriate name.

Feeling old, Vince turned off the radio.

When Vince realized the supervisor planned to ignore him, he cleared his throat and marched to the front of the desk.

"Yes?" the supervisor said.

"I don't think I should have to pay for that pallet."

The man gave him a steely look. "You're not hired to think."

"The pallet was already cracked."

"Do you deny you pulled it apart?"

"No, but we never would have used it."

"I had no opportunity to assess that." Pasty Face placed both elbows on his desk, cradling his bald head with both hands in a parody of weary patience.

Vince's eyes burned with wrath. Vince knew the supervisor hated to have his authority challenged. Logic told him to back away, but lately he hadn't been in control of himself. The events on Lostart Street had chipped away at his control. His emotions released and tumbled like a boulder down a steep incline.

"We have never used a cracked pallet," Vince said.

The small, spindly man pulled upright in his padded swivel chair and his pale face flushed. "Son, you haven't been here long enough to know what we've never done."

Vince planted his fists on the desk and restrained them with his weight. "If I were the son of a mealy-mouth jerkoff like you, I'd die from embarrassment, knowing my mother was so desperate."

The man's squinchy eyes widened as he collapsed back into the cushions of the chair. He laced manicured, nicotine-stained fingers. "Are you finished . . . ?" The word *son* hung on the man's discolored lips. "You seem to forget I have the power to suspend you *indefinitely*."

Vince straightened, shook out the fists, and felt the boulder rumbling through his chest. "You don't have power," Vince said, surprised and proud of his calm voice. He wheeled around and left the warehouse.

On the patio of the Crow's Nest, Vince slouched and sipped his third Dos XX as he glumly surveyed all the masts in the harbor poking into the overcast November sky. He had the view to himself. The tourists had gone and normal folks were at work. The lunch crowd ate downstairs.

The boulder had quit tumbling and rested now in his gut. He'd briefly considered crawling back to Pasty Face, but instead he'd come here to drown his sorrows in alcohol. He wasn't the type to go back. He had a forward-moving personality. Besides, in spite of the horrible lump in his gut, the tumble of emotion had cleared a swath through his system. A person had to make the best of whatever happened and proceed.

Of course, sitting here getting buzzed didn't make the best of it. He would have gone home if Punky had been there, but she was tromping around looking for daycare.

A small sailboat puttered from the harbor. One young man hoisted the main sail as the other manned the rudder. The boat followed the curve of the jetty into the ocean and when its rocking made him queasy, Vince knew he was a bit intoxicated. What a day to sail. They were going to get soaked. He decided to walk around the harbor to Aldo's for a burger and fries. He loved Santa Cruz, but so did too many other people. He'd have a tough time finding another job.

When Todd fell asleep in his car seat, Punky headed home. The drizzle released the smell of earth from the dry ground, but it also made her more aware of the odor of exhaust as she steered carefully along the slick Soquel Drive.

She'd had no luck. One place said they could put her on their waiting list. *A year long!* At first she'd marveled that people could have their lives planned so far in advance, but when she added her name, she realized others had signed with the same sense of why not, what could it hurt?

At another daycare, the woman had smoked while Punky talked to her. At the home of yet another woman, grit littered the worn carpet.

Exhausted from the search, Punky pulled into the apartments behind a smooth-rolling, metallic blue Cadillac Seville with PROPRTY plates. The unfamiliar car continued to the end of the drive. She extracted Todd from his car seat and protected him from the sprinkle of rain as she struggled up the step. His dead weight was getting too heavy for one arm, so she opened the door with her foot.

She took a last look at the Cadillac and then glanced nervously over her shoulder at Lefty's, glad he was gone and relieved when her door slammed securely behind her. She hoped Lefty was never unleashed on the public again—yet a sad ache filled her. No one chose to be mentally ill. It must be terrifying to feel one's faculties slipping.

Inside, she settled Todd on the bed, covering him with a flannel blanket and caressing his silky cheek with one finger. Yes, Lefty had been dealt a cruel fate, but that didn't mean he belonged around her baby.

Dragging herself to the kitchen, Punky slit open a package of ranch-grown chicken. Vince was a meat and potatoes guy. This pinkish breast represented the compromise they'd reached for tonight's dinner to celebrate her new job.

Something banged on the door and Punky dropped the chicken into the sink. Rushing to the bedroom, she peeked out the window. A grotesque face, its hair wet and plastered to its skull, the nose and lips flattened against the glass stared back at her.

She screamed.

"Punky!" The face backed away from the rain-streaked window. "It's me. Let me in."

Todd lifted his lids. She stroked his head. "It's okay, honey.

Go back to sleep. Mama's okay."

Punky waited for his eyelids to droop back down before moving to the other room.

She threw open the door. "What are you doing here?"

"God, Punky, I wasn't trying to scare you. I thought my face would look funny."

Under the greasy smell of burger and fries, Punky caught a whiff of beer. "Are you drunk? What are you doing home? Why aren't you at work?"

"I quit," Vince said gloomily. "Now can I come in?"

She left the room and returned to toss him a towel and a sweatshirt. "That's the biggest thing I own so it might fit."

"I'm sorry I scared you."

"Me, too," she said, still shaken. "But I get how fighting with a boss and getting drunk could impair your judgment."

"You sound like me, and boy is that cheerless." He dried his hair.

She laughed, hearty and full-bodied, everything suddenly seeming much better.

He smiled.

"Do you mind if I make soup instead of the fancy meal I'd planned?" she asked. "That way I can cook on automatic pilot and listen to your tale of woe at the same time." Plus the hunk of meat would be a lot more palatable that way.

"Sounds perfect." He stripped off his wet shirt revealing his six-pack abs and tugged on the sweatshirt. It pinched up under his arms. "What about your day?"

"You first." She gathered potatoes, garlic, carrot, celery, onion, a cutting board, and various spices on the counter.

As Punky diced vegetables, they swapped stories. She pulled out a cast iron kettle, heated some peanut oil, and tossed in all the vegetables.

"There's only one *logical* thing to do," she said, mocking him.

Vince laughed at her mockery.

After stirring the vegetables with a wooden spoon, she slipped her arms around him and looked up earnestly.

He was falling into her gray eyes. He was the boulder tumbling. "What's that?"

"Move in with me and take care of Todd while I start work. No commitment. Consider it a symbiotic relationship until we're both on our feet."

The fragrance of homemade food wafted past his nose and her cuddly breasts pressed his ribs. *Symbiotic*, a relationship he understood, but it scared him, too.

"A house husband?"

"I didn't propose," she said. "No commitment."

Somehow that didn't reassure him. As a matter of fact, for a moment he glimpsed the stereotyped role of the woman, keeping the house and caring for the child. It terrified him. The relationship would not be *symbiotic* at all. The orderly world of work was so much easier than the messy world of home.

"We'll have to work out some bugs," Vince said.

Cinder El

Mr. PROPRTY, John Citrino, tugged down his slick, blue warm-up jacket before sticking his slick blue legs and unsoiled athletic shoes into the light rain. He thought the attire made him look young. He bounded up the steps and rapped at the door.

Lorraine called for him to enter. She inclined her head to him. God it was a shame about her legs. She had the most spectacular face he'd ever seen, a testament to staying out of the sun, not much practiced in Southern California. Cranking those wheels had also pumped her jugs into perfection.

"I've been waiting for you for two days," she said.

"Well, I had to give the offer some thought." He glanced around for a place to sit but there was none.

"I need room to maneuver," she explained. "My friends sit on the floor."

"That's the kind of thing I'm worried about."

"My friends don't mind," she said.

"I mean the maneuvering. How are you going to get around?"

"You mean so I can do all those chores like Bobbi did?" Sarcasm laced her voice.

"I realize her recreation got a bit out of control, but that's not the issue now. The issue is whether you can do the job."

"Look around my apartment."

Someone who knew construction had lowered everything from her counters to her towel racks. All done, he assumed, without permission or permits. He nodded in approval. "So why didn't you have a ramp made?"

"Outta sight, outta mind." Lorraine whizzed to the closet, tipped a windbreaker from a dowel, and slipped it on. "Let's take a look around the place, and I'll tell you my proposals and show you my moves." She winked at him. "Let's go."

John Citrino paused.

"My boyfriend carries me."

He examined her but didn't move.

Lorraine laughed. "Okay, fine. Just go hold the door for me from the bottom."

He did as directed and watched her fly from the step. The chair whomped onto the asphalt as it had on Saturday. "I'd prefer that ramp," she said. "My chair takes a beating when I do this." She wheeled to him as he nudged the door shut.

He nodded. "Okay. How did you get this door to open outward?"

"Oh, I manage." She laughed. "No pun intended."

The rain was letting up. He crossed to the charred remains of Mrs. Bean's place, yanked down the caution tape, and mounted the steps. "First I want to check out this place."

"The firemen told us not to go near it." Lorraine stayed far back. "Walls fall outward."

John Citrino inspected her as though she'd failed a test, stepped into the house, and yelped. "God dammit all to hell! Lorraine, get over her and help me. Prove you can *manage*."

Lorraine eyed the landing, both smaller and more elevated than hers. Plus it was wet. She inhaled deeply, took a run at it, and popped up, stopping just short of the caved-in floor. One of John Citrino's legs had plunged through the blackened wood and the other had buckled beneath him. When he tried to lever his leg from the hole, the charred wood cracked beneath his weight.

"Jesus, there's nothing under here."

Soot blackened him everywhere. He looked like Al Jolson down in his dramatic pose to sing the National Anthem.

Lorraine's eyes twinkled. "Are you hurt?"

"I don't think so, but wherever I lean, it feels like it'll cave in."

Citrino yelped. "And I heard a rat."

"Can you reach my chair?"

"I don't know."

"Well I have an idea. We may as well give it a try. If you fall through, it's not far to the ground."

"Thanks a lot," he snapped.

"You're not very grateful. I could let you flounder around in the charcoal and be eaten by rats."

"Okay, God dammit. Tell me what to do."

She resisted reaching for the contractual agreement she'd typed. She maneuvered a tight turn and backed her chair as close to the wreckage as seemed safe. "I'm going to lock the brakes. Then I'll grab the railing. If you can stretch your hands to the chair and your free leg to the concrete, you should be able to hoist yourself. Just don't grab the walls."

The rain slowed to a drizzle. Bucky pranced toward them holding a purple umbrella. Dudu tugged at the leash, an imperial-purple ribbon bouncing against his white forehead.

Citrino humphed as he thrust his body forward. The chair jerked but held as he caught it and lifted himself over to the sill. "Thanks." He looked down at the fluffy dog pissing at the base of the rail. "Hey!" He flailed his blackened arms.

"Calm down, John," Lorraine said. "Dudu's been urinating there for years. His partner is the brave and fearless Bucky who stopped the homicidal maniac the night of the fire, or did you miss that news item?"

"Dance, Dudu," Bucky commanded. The dog stood on its hind legs and turned in a full circle. Then he lay on the wet blacktop and spun his body. "He is break dancing." Bucky beamed from beneath his umbrella.

"That's pretty neat." Citrino rolled his eyes.

"I wouldn't do that if I were you," Lorraine whispered. "You look enough like a minstrel as it is."

"I have a ghetto blaster," Bucky said. "When it is sunny, I'm gonna take Dudu to the Mall, see if we can make some money."

"Great," Citrino said.

Bucky glowed. Sarcasm fell wide of his small world. "You're really dirty," Bucky said to Citrino as the dog flipped, landed on all fours and shook muddy grit from his white fur. Dudu stretched the leash. "Bye," Bucky said.

Lorraine smiled after them. It was funny how, over time, Bucky's speech defect had vanished into the background.

As Citrino carefully pulled the charred door into place, a mewling noise issued from the sub-floor.

Lorraine cocked her head and twisted toward Citrino. "Did you hear something?"

"Like what?"

"I don't know. Maybe there are rats down there." She rolled her chair off the landing. The thud shuddered her bones. To manage the complex effectively, she might need ramps to all the units, but she kept that idea to herself. "You can wash at my place but I can't do much about your track-suit."

They crossed the driveway behind Dudu, who had paused to trickle on Lorraine's water-meter pipe.

After the humbled Citrino had scrubbed, Lorraine proposed they get back to business.

Citrino had never dreamed he'd be doing so much work here even when Bobbi called about the fire. He'd imagined surveying the damage, okaying Bobbi's choice of contractor, and then returning to LA until the insurance claim was settled. He'd brought a gram of coke up with him and rented a room at the quaint Capitola Hotel, planning to spend a couple nights licking premium flake from Bobbi's vaginal lips. Instead he'd gotten this mess.

"I want you to see Mrs. Bean's new place," Lorraine said.

"Huh?"

On their way out, Lorraine explained how she and Cecile had installed Mrs. Bean in Florence's apartment. "Now I'm sure you have insurance for the structure, but Mrs. Bean didn't have renter's insurance. She's been left with nothing."

"I'm not running an assistance program," he grumbled.

"She has social security." The wheelchair whizzed over the wet asphalt, splashing his ruined shoes. Citrino's pants swished-swished as he tried to keep up.

"Cecile and I donated blankets for last night," the woman said, "and some of Florence's dishes haven't been packed. I suggest we put Florence's personal effects in storage, although I doubt anyone will claim them, and leave the functional stuff to charity, if you get my drift." She nodded at the apartment, but Citrino's gaze turned away, down the drive where a man was pressing his face up to a bedroom window.

"Don't worry," Lorraine said. "That's not our resident killer. Vince is Punky's lover."

"But I thought I heard someone scream," he stammered.

"He just startled her," Lorraine said. "We'll soon have another vacancy to worry about beside Lefty Hunt's." They were stopped below the step of what was apparently now Mrs. Bean's new home, Florence's former place.

"I don't follow."

Lorraine pointed at Punky's apartment, to which the guy named Vince had gained admittance. "Those two aren't going to keep paying two rents now they're sleeping together."

"This is a weird place."

"It's all yours," Lorraine snickered. She stretched her arms wide to embrace the whole weird community. "I'll wait here. It's a bit much popping up and down these steps."

"What do you want me to do?"

"I want you to meet Mrs. Bean and check out the condition

of the apartment. And, just in case you still have reservations about switching managers, I want you to bring out the Macy's bag by the door."

John knocked, waited and turned to leave.

"Knock some more."

This woman was really bossy. Citrino scratched his head. That could be a good quality in a manager. He knocked again and after a pause Mrs. Bean drew the deadbolt and cracked the door the width of the chain.

The old woman peered at him through the slit. "Who are you?" Her eyes squinted at his besmudged clothes.

"He's the owner," Lorraine said.

In slow motion Mrs. Bean admitted him and in fast motion he exited. Only a sad, desperate person would want to stay in that smelly, water-stained hole. These units had never been billed as luxury apartments, but the state of disrepair shocked him.

He clutched the Macy's bag. "What's the deal with this?"

"Look in it."

"There's not much to see, just a crystal bowl with a chain and wedding band in it."

"And how do those items strike you?"

He thought for a moment. "Florence's objects of value?" he guessed. "From the looks of that dump, probably her only objects of value." He closed the bag. "Now why don't you explain and quit leading me around by the nose."

"Funny you should mention being led around by the nose. Who packed Florence's stuff?"

"Bobbi."

"I'd suggest she didn't mean to store these items."

He pondered the implication. It made sense.

"You're not the only person she's been ripping off. Bobbi is our resident thief."

What Happened to Lefty

I picked up the local newspaper from a table in the teachers' lounge. The headline popped from the second page, but I choose to save and savor the piece over coffee. As I drove home, I averted my eyes from the passenger seat where the paper lay open to the story: Man Accidentally Slays Neighbor.

The distraction was dangerous. The first rain loosened oil residue onto the freeway surface and my bug's old tires slipped along the surface.

When I reached my apartment, the Seville was parked in front of Lorraine's. It barely caused palpitations. As my kettle heated, I watched the neighborhood through rain dripping from the eaves.

After I prepared my coffee, I sat at my desk and read.

During the confusion of a fire Thursday night at 666 Lostart Street, William "Lefty" Hunt, 25, allegedly stabbed and killed his fifty-eight-year-old neighbor Florence Marie Nissenbaum. According to eyewitnesses, "Lefty" Hunt was attempting to stab his neighbor Vincent Shields with a butcher knife when he accidentally stabbed Nissenbaum in the stomach. Neighbors and local firemen at the scene said Hunt claimed he'd been commanded by God to kill the devil. According to one neighbor, Hunt had been enraged by jealousy over Shields' affair with another tenant in the apartments.

A fireman reported that Shields had restrained Florence Nissenbaum from dashing to the burning apartment to rescue a cat when Hunt stabbed her instead of Shields. Residents disarmed Hunt and firemen called the Sheriff's Office. Nissenbaum suffered internal hemorrhaging from the single stab wound and was pronounced dead on arrival at Dominican Hospital at 10:37 p.m.

According to Sergeant Munoz of the County Sheriff's Department, Hunt seemed stunned and disoriented when arrested. "He didn't make any phone calls when we booked him," Munoz stated. Hunt spent a quiet weekend in the Santa Cruz County Jail, awaiting arraignment.

"Enraged by jealousy." I wondered which neighbor had given the reporter that precious tidbit. I hadn't even seen a reporter, but then the weekend had been full of distractions.

Most likely Lefty would be assigned a public defender who would ask for a reduced sentence, or enter a diminished capacity plea.

Well that was the end of my coffee and my break. Picking up a stack of essays, I thought of Lefty at the Santa Cruz County Jail, relinquishing his shoes, belt, and identity. *His identity.* That was a laugh. He didn't have one, at least not a solid, secure one, but then I wasn't sure I had one of those either.

A Change of Heart

"I thought you were glad you told your supervisor off," Punky said, nestling against Vince's shoulder. Behind the futon on the windowsill she'd accumulated and lit every candle she owned. A dozen fragrant lights flickered around them.

"I was. I mean, I am," Vince said. "I wouldn't trade the look on his face for anything. But I lost. When I left the warehouse, he probably laughed."

"Why would he laugh? He'll have to interview people to replace you, and I doubt he'll find anyone as good."

"He'll love replacing me, Punky. That's exactly what the guy wanted."

"Well, you didn't say you quit, did you?" She snuggled again into the crook of his arm. Vince put his arm around her but his body remained taut.

"That's what I was thinking. I could report to work tomorrow and see what happens. Check with Payroll first and see if I'm still listed, and if I am, simply go to work. See if the guy has balls enough to tell me I'm fired. If I've already been fired or he tells me I'm fired, I'll check into the procedure for a grievance. I need to have a job."

"I guess this is one of the big bugs in my plan," Punky said.

"Yeah." He relaxed now that he'd got that out. "I'm sorry to disappoint you."

"I'm disappointed, but not in you, Vince. I think you're

doing the right thing."

He leaned over and kissed her. When he started to dis-engage, she initiated her own kiss. His hand slipped into her kimono and his body unwound a bit more, the weight sinking into the futon and floor. "I'll help with Todd when I can. If I'm suspended, I can babysit until I'm reinstated. If you can't find a sitter tomorrow, you could ask for a schedule that includes weekends and evenings."

She sighed. "We'd never see each other if I did that."

"If we're living together, we'd still see more of each other than we do now."

She turned on her side to be more accessible and her hair spilled over her shoulder and brushed his bare chest. "Oh. Are you still interested in that part of the proposal?"

"I thought it was a plan, not a proposal," he said. "Don't use that word, it scares me."

She laughed. He loved the sound of her unabashed hap-piness. Her fingers toyed absently with his belly button. It was almost an outy, with skin rounded in the shallow indentation of the firm surface.

"But," he said.

She lifted her eyes.

"I want you to move to my place."

She frowned.

"My place won't look like it does now when you get done moving in." He snatched her fingers as though catching a lizard. "You should be glad it's bare and there's room for your stuff."

"Yes, but that's why you should move. You have less stuff."

"I have a yard."

"It's on the street."

"We can fence it," he said.

"You're making this hard."

"I'm making it easy, Punky." He waggled her small, soft fingers. "Did you know my apartment has a very small second bedroom?"

"When do I move in?" She pulled loose from his grip and tickled his sides.

He couldn't help himself. He'd always been ticklish. He laughed, full out, unrestrained. He hadn't laughed like this since he was a kid.

Punky laughed with him, her cheeks flushed pink, like roses in the candlelight. She stopped attacking his ribs. "How much notice do we have to give?"

Cecile

The students had fallen into the groove and were not yet antsy about Thanksgiving. On an international scale, El Salvador ordered a U.S. envoy to stop criticizing its violations of human rights. That squabbling between the United States and El Salvador had been continuous since the start of its civil war. Ongoing international power struggles hardly grabbed people's attention like the cyanide-laced Tylenol in October, even though our government was taking the side of a regime that caused people to disappear.

For me, a person reappeared. After the second bell shrilled, Rosaura sprang into the room, her arms out-flung. "I'm back!"

Her hair had grown an amazing amount during the short time she'd been gone. Wild dark curls touched her shoulders. She had a new pair of black pants and had taken up the punk style of gathering the legs tight using a series of safety pins.

"I thought your family moved to Arizona." I said, which did not begin to reveal how happy I was to see her.

"They let me come back to stay with my aunt." She glanced around the room. "Where do I sit?"

My class had more students than Annette's, and after Rosaura left, Annette had moved out Rosaura's desk to clear a little space.

Annette gathered her materials and rose from the teacher's desk. "You can sit here for now."

Rosaura pranced over and seated herself like she was queen for the day. I marveled again that with her transient life, Rosaura read at grade level. *Amazing.* The test score at the beginning of the year hardly revealed how smart she must be.

Even though it was weeks until Christmas, a smile slipped across my lips.

The class had read *Cat-About-Town* by James Herriot, a nice, but completely inappropriate, story. Animal stories filled their literature text. The stories may have been okay if my freshmen class was comprised of freshmen, but more than half the students were sophomore and junior "repeaters." They didn't cotton to animal stories, although a rousing discussion ensued of various tortures for cats. One particular braggart named Baltazar admitted that a cat prowling in his yard meant target practice.

I persuaded other students to talk about the losses of their pets and how that felt. Next I proposed the not-so-hypothetical possibility Baltazar could have caused the animals' deaths.

Baltazar stiffened. "I didn't do that."

Rosaura lunged up from the teacher's desk. "How do you know?"

Baltazar wouldn't soon forget the way Rosaura's eyes blazed at him. At least, I hoped not.

By the time I'd pulled into the carport beside Mrs. Bean's Dodge Dart, my high had disintegrated into shame. I had completely manipulated the situation to corner Baltazar.

If Rosaura hadn't beaten me to the punch, I would have nailed him with exactly the same question. But the victory I'd felt in trapping him had been short-lived. My assurance I was on the "right" side only made me feel more fascist. Teaching was a tricky business, requiring constant vigilance over one's motives and methods.

Still, a warm glow filled my heart at the return of my ally Rosaura. One student could transform a room. Could transform what it felt like for me to go to work. One little connection.

With my desire to carry everything from my car in one trip, I loaded my arms. As I clutched my purse with my knees to free a hand for the mail, Lorraine, with her impeccable timing, called to me.

"Come here. I have to tell someone the good news."

"Just a minute." I opened my door, spilled the stuff from my arms, glanced at the junk mail, picked up my purse and crossed to Lorraine's window.

"Why don't you come in?"

"This is an occasion," I said.

The only large piece of furniture in her apartment was the table in front of the window, equipped with typewriter, a cup full of pens and pencils, a pencil sharpener, a legal pad, and basic reference books. Lorraine reversed from the table.

I eyed Lorraine's full pant legs, which ended in a pair of regular shoes. "Where'd you get those?" I was as bad as the worst blurter in my class.

"Oh, I've had these legs for a long time," she said. "You can either sit on the floor or lift down the folding chair from the top of my closet."

"The floor's fine." I sank onto the wood. I gawked at the jeans bent before me.

"If my pants were looser, I'd show you my prosthesis," she said.

"Why don't you usually wear your . . ." I fumbled for the right word, "legs?"

"If you knew how long it took me to get dressed today, you wouldn't ask."

"Can you walk in those?"

"Not really. I'm much faster in my chair. My boyfriend has one artificial leg and he can do everything a person with two legs can, but for me it's a major chore to hoist myself onto these things. It's hard for people to understand why I go around without them, but everyone who cares about me will find out sooner or later that they're phony anyway. Mostly I use them as chair filler when I'm going out with someone who might be self-conscious about my handicap."

"Like John Citrino?" I propped my back against her wall and bumped my head on a picture. Everything on her walls hung low.

"Right," she beamed. "He agreed to make me manager. Tonight we celebrate and work out some details."

I raised an eyebrow.

"Don't worry. I'm not his type."

"You're female."

She laughed. "Listen, Cecile, to my plan." She brushed her hair away from her face. Mascara highlighted her luminous eyes and pale lipstick glistened on her lips. A black silk blouse emphasized the creamy paleness of her complexion. Crows feet tiptoed from her eyes, but she was a well-preserved beauty.

"John agreed to keep the rents the same. We're all used to them anyway. But now that he'll actually receive what we're paying, he'll use the difference to fix these places, starting with Florence's—or rather Mrs. Bean's. Tonight I'll suggest an advance so I can start right away."

"Where are you going for dinner?"

"Chaminade-Whitney."

"Be careful, Lorraine."

Even in my short time here, I'd heard of the place. Chaminade-Whitney was swanky, perched like a palace on private, wooded acreage above Santa Cruz. It wasn't a restaurant I associated with a business dinner.

"He's not going to do anything I don't want him to do," she said enigmatically.

"What about your boyfriend?"

She laughed at me. "God, Cecile, you're such a prude."

Prude. The tag surprised rather than offended me. I'd never been called a prude before.

"We have to start working on that," Lorraine said.

Probably not a bad idea.

Prude reminded me of prune, something drying up against a hard, inner pit.

"But first you need to change into some work clothes."

"Huh?"

"I need your help."

All our previous adventures—breaking into Florence's, taking on Bobbi Headland—had been thrilling. I stood up. "Give me a second."

I returned in five minutes, wearing my Oshkosh overalls over one of Angelo's old shirts.

"So, what's up?" I asked.

"Follow me."

She led me out of the apartment, down the step, and across the asphalt. She stopped in front of Mrs. Bean's burned-out apartment. My body jittered. Surely Lorraine did not expect me to go in there. The structure was unsound.

"You're just going to open the door," she said.

"That's dangerous."

"John opened it. Everything was fine."

Then why don't you open it, I thought, but her handicap prevented me. Lorraine was not the type to ask for help if she didn't need it. Whatever needed doing, I could probably do it more easily than she could.

"Why would anyone go in there?" I asked. "There can't be anything left."

"You're not going in, per se."

"Per se?"

"If you open the door, you'll see a hole in the floor where John fell through."

"So everything was fine, huh?" My voice sounded angry. "Exactly the reason we shouldn't be fooling around here."

"Just crack the door a little and make some kissing sounds like you're calling a cat."

Comprehension slowly dawned. "You think that cat survived the fire?"

"John heard some animal noise," Lorraine said. "He dismissed it as rats and I didn't give it much thought until later."

"How would that even be possible?" But I already had an idea. "There was that hole under Mrs. Bean's table," I mumbled. "Like an opening for a heating duct, but there was no duct."

"I didn't know that," Lorraine said. "So there is a way the cat could have gotten under the floor."

"And if he . . . ."

"She."

"If she was below the fire . . . . " The heat would be traveling up. As I was. I mounted the step, turned the doorknob, and pushed.

The door didn't budge. A sense of urgency swept through me. I could be heroic like the firemen. I pressed against the blackened wood and made loud cat-calling tongue noises. "Kitty," I called. "Kitty, kitty, kitty."

A scratching noise. But maybe it was a rat.

"Kitty, kitty, kitty?"

A pathetic mewl answered.

"Oh my God, she's there," I said to Lorraine. I slammed my shoulder against the charred wood. The door stayed stuck. Black soot covered the sleeve of my shirt. I put my shoulder to the door again with my focus on the frame. The stuck section was at knee level. "Do you have a hammer?"

"Of course," Lorraine said. "Bottom kitchen drawer on the right."

I jogged across the drive and leapt up the step to Lorraine's. The hammer was easy to locate and I was back at the jammed door in under a minute. I turned the knob, shouldered the door, and hammered the wedged spot.

The wood splintered. The door cracked open an inch and caught. I peeked through the slit. "Where are you, kitty?"

"That noise would have scared away a pitbull," Lorraine groused.

I got down on my hands and knees and peered through the

slot. No doubt charcoal smeared my face like war paint.

Splintered floorboards blocked the door from opening further. That must have been where Citrino fell through. But he'd been able to shut the door. Had the cat caused more wood to break?

I put my nose to the crack. I kissed and clucked and called.

A head popped from the hole, green eyes appearing huge with the multi-colored fur matted flat against its head. Cobwebs draped from its whiskers. The mangy, soaked bundle padded to the crack in the door and mewed at me.

How would I get her out?

The windows remained in tact. The firemen had said this was a good thing, restricting oxygen to the fire. If I broke one now, would the cat come out? How could I prevent it from getting cut?

"This is a sorry mess," I muttered to Lorraine. "Any ideas?"

Lorraine rolled along the drive. "How about this sub-floor vent?"

The vent opening was big enough for a cat to pass through, but paint caked the screws holding the screen in place. I doubted I could muscle them off with a screwdriver and if I put a drill to them would the vibration bring a wall down on me?

I climbed back to the door. The cat cried piteously.

The wood had splintered pretty easily. "Stand back, baby," I said to the cat. An unnecessary warning. At the first bang, it sprang out of sight.

The door didn't break.

But the wood behind it cracked. The splintered floor acting as a doorstop gave way and the door opened a foot.

Down on all fours, I coaxed the cat. It pulled itself from the hole in the floor, padded across the burned floor, and nuzzled my hand with its damp head.

I cradled the dirty furball against my overalls. She started to purr. My heart melted.

"I think she's found a new friend," Lorraine said.

"But isn't she Mrs. Bean's?"

"Mrs. Bean inherited three other cats with Florence's apartment."

As I snuggled the mess, Lorraine was already making plans. "Florence left behind plenty of cat food and litter. I'll get someone to bring it over. You should take your baby home and clean her up."

Breaking the Image

The next day, Ruben lumbered up to me before class, his black eyes snapping.

Rosaura pushed up to the lectern beside him, the corners of her mouth wiggling as she tried to suppress a smile. Others students circled me.

Ruben stuck a sheet of binder paper under my nose. "Read this."

It was clearly a challenge of some sort. I looked down at the paper and tried to sound out the word formed by seven block letters. "Tahnsaltso."

"No, no, no." Ruben shook his bush of black hair. "Read the letters one at a time."

The students' excitement palpitated around me. "T. N. S. L. T. S. O." I enunciated clearly.

They giggled, but Ruben said sternly, "You have to read them faster."

The bell rang but the kids remained grouped around me, pressing closer until I could feel their warmth and smell their bodies.

I didn't tell them to take their seats, but rather complied with Ruben's instructions, starting to get it. The T.N.S. made sense.

"*Tienes*?" You have? I guessed.

Ruben's head bobbed with excitement.

"*El?*" The.

I studied the last part. I didn't know any Spanish word that sounded like T.S.O. But I uttered it anyway.

The group laughed, but Ruben was a strict teacher. A stubby finger with a dirty nail poked the paper. "Say it all together."

"*Tienes el tee-es-o?*"

The group howled.

I smiled unsurely, my face hot. "What does that mean?"

A voice came from the teacher's desk. "*Tieso* means stiff. Sounds like some slangy version of, 'You have a hard-on.'"

At the sound of Annette's voice the students scrambled to their seats. But I was sick of all this, of feeling like someone else was running my classroom. Instead of moving to the day's lesson, I turned, wiggled my brows, and asked Ruben, "*Tienes el tieso?*" Do you have a hard-on?

He jumped up from his seat, puffed up his chest, and turned in a slow 180, addressing the whole class. "*Todo el tiempo, muchachas.*" All the time, girls.

At the end of class, I gathered my supplies to dash to the next classroom.

"Slow down, Kiddo."

I halted in front of Annette's desk like a delinquent student, awaiting a lecture.

She studied me.

My face flushed. I'd been an idiot. Even if the slang Spanish barely made sense, I had been totally inappropriate to mention "the stiff." I had no tenure. That kind of stupidity could cost me my job.

"They played a joke on you."

Well, yeah.

Annette grinned. "They like you."

After school, Annette asked me if I wanted to join her and the Bobbsey Twins, Lily and Marge, for drinks at Severino's.

"It's a fairly quiet bar, out of town, about halfway to Santa Cruz."

Since I'd survived my first couple of months and Annette had witnessed the first period students *liking* me, they apparently felt I was now safe. "I don't know," I said. "Things are hectic."

I thought of the cat in my unfamiliar apartment, left alone all day. I'd cleaned her with a damp towel. Then she'd gobbled food and snuggled up on my bed for the night, where she'd remained in a ball when I left for work. I should get home.

"I hate to tell you this, Kiddo," Annette said, "but I've been teaching seventeen years, and things are always hectic. Give yourself a break. You have a three-day weekend coming up to recoup from the big adventure."

"Okay." I might not receive another invitation. "Veteran's Day weekend comes in the nick of time, doesn't it?"

"You got that right."

As the four of us sat around the bar table, we politely chatted about the death of Leonid Brezhnev and what we thought would happen in the Soviet Union.

I nursed a brandy alexander. Lily and Marge both sipped the same type of light beer as if to reinforce their Bobbsey Twins moniker. Even up close, they looked astoundingly alike—both short, chubby and blonde with apple cheeks and blue eyes. They commuted to work together, ate lunch together, and sat together at faculty meetings. I couldn't help the thought that either they'd been separated at birth, or they were a couple who started to look alike over time.

Annette drank Jack Daniels neat, a tough drink for a tough lady. As a second round of drinks loosened us up, Annette made no bones about her brazen attitude toward men. "They're good for one thing."

But our conversation didn't linger on men or our personal lives.

"Do you know why the DeLorean is called a vanity car?" Annette asked us.

We all obliged her with, "No, why?"

"It has a mirror in the glove compartment." This was a reference to the famous automobile engineer John DeLorean's arrest for drug trafficking. Cocaine.

We chuckled, grateful for the light note.

"How about those grosser-than-gross jokes the kids are telling?" Lily wrinkled her nose. "Do you want to hear the one I heard today?"

"Okay," I said.

"What's grosser than gross?" Lily obliged.

"What?" I asked.

"A truckful of dead babies."

My brandy alexander smacked onto the table. I'd heard other grosser-than-gross jokes before, but this one landed a blow to my stomach.

Marge nudged my shoulder. "You're supposed to ask what's grosser than that?"

I couldn't speak, so Marge jumped in. "What's grosser than that?"

"A live one at the bottom," Lily said.

Marge and Annette emitted groans.

"Do you want to know what's grosser than that?" Lily asked.

Annette must have sensed my discomfort because she said, "Please, Lily, we are trying to drink here." She motioned over the waitress.

I begged off on a third round, ordering a cup of coffee, so I could hang out and sober up. The talk slipped into gossipy stuff about certain male teachers.

"I feel it's my duty to warn you we have some notorious skirt chasers on the staff," Annette said, "and, Kiddo, you may even be young enough to attract them."

The alcohol emboldened me. "Kiddo?" I said. "It's time for a new name."

Annette leaned back in her chair as though pressed. Lily and Marge fell silent. "Okay," Annette said. "How about Boss?"

"How about Cecile?"

"Sure thing, Ki . . . Cecile."

"And I can guess who the guys are." I rattled off three names.

Annette raised her eyebrows. "I'm impressed."

"They're pretty obvious."

"Rumor has it that they even fraternize with students."

"Why doesn't someone report it?" I asked.

"You need hard evidence to make that kind of charge," Annette said.

"So to speak," Lily quipped.

We all laughed.

As I sat in the bar, I thought about the women at work. The two with husbands and families remained ephemeral characters who arrived after school started and disappeared before the end of the day. All the full-time women remained unencumbered by relationships. Besides Annette, Lily, Marge and myself, the department contained two others, a widow with grown children and a nun-like, middle-aged woman. We all bore the mark of dedicated female English teachers, a certain sexlessness, or, at least, the absence of the demands of a man and family.

I yearned to do an excellent job, but I shuddered at the apparent cost. *The old maid school marm.* Like most stereotypes, it embraced a measure of truth.

By the time I got home, it was dark. A day that had started with laughter ended with sadness.

But then, carrying my load of stuff, I opened my door. The cat greeted me and wrapped around my leg.

The next time I went to Annette's classroom, she was standing in the doorway. A second lectern hulked up in the front, a rolling one with shelves in the back.

"That's for you, Kiddo," she said. "So you have a place to

store things."

A spot to organize materials before class started! The difference this would make in my life was immeasurable. Gratitude welled up in me. I turned toward Annette. "Thank you so much."

She flapped a hand at me, gathered up her papers, left the room, and stayed gone the whole class period.

After school on Veteran's Day proper, I saw Lorraine again.

"I thought you'd be off," she called to me. This sounded like an accusation. Perhaps she was rankled by the lack of observance.

"We roll the holiday into the weekend." I dumped my load into the apartment and strolled to her window. The damp cold penetrated my turtleneck and skirt. I rubbed my arms to stay warm, but she didn't invite me in.

"Ask about my hot date." I could hear a wink in her voice.

"How was it?"

"Citrino asked me to marry him," she said.

"Really?"

"Cecile," she said, "did you know they're removing the word gullible from the dictionary?"

I hesitated. "Right."

"A lot has happened," she said. "Vince came over today and gave notice on Punky's apartment. They're moving in together. Just as I thought."

The news made me wistful. I couldn't help but wonder what would have happened if I'd responded to Vince. "He was off today?" I said to maintain the conversational flow even though I was starting to shiver.

"He's off indefinitely, but he's filed a grievance." Lorraine told me what had happened with Vince. "He's taking care of Todd and searching for day care. That means two vacancies to fill, but I have someone coming to look at Lefty's tomorrow. He's a friend of my boyfriend's, a sous-chef up at Chaminade-Whitney. I combined a little business with all that pleasure," she teased me. "I got Florence's and Lefty's stuff put in storage today and tomorrow I have painters coming to Mrs. Bean's."

"I guess you got the advance you wanted." I vigorously massaged my arms.

"John Citrino's a pussycat," she said. "It's no wonder Bobbi got away with the shit she did."

"I thought you said he loved his money, that he was capable of shooting her."

"Oh, he does love money, but he's smart enough to know a person has to maintain property at some minimal level. He has a broker's license."

"I'm freezing," I said.

"Well, since you're off tomorrow, why don't you drop by for scones and coffee?"

"What time?"

"About ten?"

"I can manage that."

I knew, however, that I'd sleep around the clock as I usually did at the end of a school week. My dreams were less predictable.

A man falls from the sky. His name is John DeLorean. He has curly dark hair, blue eyes, and a big dick. He is naked and wants to make love with me. We frolick in my bed, on my desk in the English Office, in Mrs. Bean's charred apartment, on the Golden Gate Bridge, moving effortlessly through a kaleidoscope of places in one continuous fuck.

Mac

At ten o'clock I did not smell any coffee at Lorraine's nor did I see any scones. The cat had awakened me at six by pushing its head against my face. I would have gladly dreamed a couple more hours. Now I had bags under my eyes and didn't appreciate the delay in getting some food in my belly.

"Malcolm's bringing the scones, and the coffee will be ready shortly."

"I didn't know someone else was coming," I griped.

"The guy to see the apartment," Lorraine explained. "I told you about him." She rolled into her kitchen.

"If I'd known I was going to meet a stranger, I would have dolled up a bit." I picked at the pills on the gray wool sweater pulled over my blue turtleneck. Old blue jeans completed my ensemble.

The fragrance of coffee floated like a warm, billowy cloud from the kitchen.

"Cream or sugar?" Lorraine asked.

"Just cream. Want some help?"

"It would be easier if you got your own cup."

The kitchen resembled a kindergarten room with all the furniture adjusted to a different perspective on the world. Lorraine had an old gas stove like mine with reachable knobs in the front, but in her chair she could use only the front burners.

I took my mug of coffee and sat on the bare living room

floor. The rap on the door didn't wait for a response. In strode a magnificent set of legs. Long-toed feet reposed in sandals in mid-November. Ankles protruded delicately but muscles corded and bulged from bulky tibia and fibula. These were not the calves of a body builder, but of an innately strong person— elemental legs. I could imagine them reconstructed from an anthropological dig.

"Hi," the man boomed, calling my eyes to cornflower blue, twinkling ones. He carried a towel-covered plate on his finger- tips. When Lorraine rode into the room, he stooped and gave her a resounding kiss on the lips and a crushing one-armed hug. "Hi ya, baby," he said cheerfully. "Has anyone told you today that you're beautiful?"

Sudden and unaccountable jealousy surged through me. The guy's energy warmed the whole room. No wonder he wore sandals in November; he was a walking boiler room.

Malcolm didn't stay fixed in place long enough for Lorraine to introduce us. "These puppies are still warm," he announced, whizzing by Lorraine and into her kitchen as though he owned the place. As dishes rattled, I mouthed to Lorraine, "I'm interested."

She stared at me blankly. When Malcolm had shown up, I'd thought her motive for inviting me patently apparent, but I'd either misjudged, or Lorraine couldn't read lips.

Malcolm returned with coffee in one hand and three small plates resting on the table of his forearm. Short, fine blond hair capriciously rearranged itself as he bent to hand each of us a serving.

"Beside the scone, you'll find Devon's cream," he intoned like a professional waiter as he settled on the floor. "I'm not one for rich stuff," he switched to his own voice, "but normal people love it."

The bright eyes turned to me. I busied myself with slath- ering Devon's cream on my scone with a knife he'd thoughtfully provided for each of us. "I'm Malcolm." His irascible eyebrows that looked like part of an Einstein disguise danced melodramatically up and down. "But most people call me Mac."

"I'm Cecile," I said, trying to mimic his brows. "But most people call me Ms. Knutsen."

"She's a teacher," Lorraine said, not apologizing for the lack of introductions.

I self-consciously sampled the scone, savoring the sweet, white cream and flavor bursts from dried fruits. *Currants?*

Mac watched me as he munched his plain scone, crumbs collecting about his mouth and sprinkling his black shirt. "Do you like it?" he inquired, as though his soul depended on pleasing the ones he served.

"Nirvana," I purred.

"Cecile, I was wondering if you'd do me a favor?" Lorraine asked.

"You can always ask."

"Would you show Malcolm the available apartment, save my wheelchair the trauma of banging off the step?"

I glared at her. She must have read my lips after all, but the obviousness of this move embarrassed me. She had no shame, either, about using her handicap to manipulate people. Maybe she felt it evened the score.

"When are you going to get a ramp?" Mac asked.

"Immediately, now that I'm manager. The problem is how to construct one that doesn't protrude too far into the driveway."

"Piece of cake," Mac stated. "I can build it. All you have to do is put a turn in it."

"It's harder than that, Malcolm. I'd get stuck in a ninety-degree angle."

"Show me what you need, buy me the wood, and I'll build it."

Mac collected the plates and rose. "Let's go look at that place. I'm anxious to get out of the St. George."

When we went out the door, we encountered Bucky and

Dudu leaving the water meter pipes. Today Dudu sported a vibrant orange ribbon.

"Hi ya." Mac greeted them. "Aren't you the guy and the dancing dog from down on Pacific Avenue?"

"Yes! Yes!" Bucky said, excited to be recognized. "Watch this." Bucky commanded Dudu to dance and the dog obediently performed.

"Fantastic!" Mac proclaimed. "Outta sight."

"It's better with music," Bucky demurred.

"I live at the St. George, so I know all the acts on the street. I like yours the best."

Bucky glowed.

As we made our way along the drive, Mrs. Bean parted her curtains to watch us pass. Malcolm waved and beamed at her like a golden sun.

Down the road, Vince carried a box from Punky's.

"Hey, man, you need a hand?" Mac said.

"Naw, we're doing this bit by bit." Vince gazed approvingly at Mac. "Thanks."

I unlocked the door to Lefty's, feeling dejected. On the way, Mac had focused on everyone except me. What I'd taken as flirtation at Lorraine's was obviously only his usual, outgoing behavior.

The apartment seemed perfectly anonymous. The floor plan duplicated mine, with the same new carpet and knotty pine in the small kitchen. Lefty's belongings had been removed and the place purged of any vestiges of his personality.

Mac beelined to the kitchen. "Gas stove," he noted. "*Muy importante*. I couldn't fix you a proper gourmet meal on an electric one."

Mac the Knife

Since the St. George Hotel stood less on ceremony than most establishments and required only a week's notice, and since Mac had pared his life to fit into one of its rooms, he transported all his possessions in two trips the following Friday. By Saturday, he was ready to serve me the promised dinner.

I gussied up for the occasion in my red, black and white silk dress and invested in a pair of black nylons with seams.

He threw open the door as I climbed his steps with my offering of chardonnay.

"Hey, gorgeous, I hope you like steak because I bought you a fourteen-ounce sirloin, and I exchanged shifts with a buddy to have this night off to prepare it for you."

My heart plummeted. I hadn't eaten red meat in eight years. I could manage a bit for the sake of politeness, but the sight of a huge slab of beef would nauseate me.

"Just kidding," Mac kissed my cheek and received the bottle of wine. "I know you don't eat steak."

"How do you know that?"

"If you ate a bit of succulent, juicy, rare beef, you wouldn't look anemic and malnutritioned."

Before I could even be offended or correct malnutritioned with the word malnourished, he hurried into his kitchen, adding over his shoulder, "And this is Santa Cruz."

"No it isn't." I hovered at the kitchen entry, as he efficiently popped the cork and poured each of us a water glass of wine.

"I can tell we're going to have a wonderful time," he said cryptically.

The aromas of fish and cooking rice permeated the apartment. He tipped his glass back and forth. "Good legs." He peered at me through his glass. He swirled and sniffed the wine. "Excellent nose. I propose a toast."

"I have one." I touched my glass to his. "Here's to you and here's to me; may we never disagree, but if we do, to hell with you, and here's to me."

"Good toast." He swallowed a bit. "And good wine." He turned back to his work. Open bottles of soy sauce, plum sauce, five spice, and sesame seed oil and a bag of blanched almonds filled the small, splattered counter.

"Let me tell you about sirloin steak." Mac crunched across rice spilled on the floor and placed a red bell pepper and green onions on a cutting board. "Back in the time of the Crusades, King Richard returned victorious and naturally a great feast was prepared for him."

With expert thwacks, Mac diced the vegetables. "Richard's chef wanted to make something outrageous for the king, so instead of cooking off a hindquarter or a whole pig as was the custom, this chef cut out just the tenderest loin meat to cook." Mac leaned and pulled a beat-up plastic bowl from the under-the-counter refrigerator and added the red bell pepper and green onion to an Oriental noodle salad. "Anyway, King Richard loved the meat so much he knighted it, and that's why we have Sir Loin of Beef."

"Is that true?"

He shrugged, raised his whimsical eyebrows, and wiped his hands on his 501 Levi's. They hung perfectly on him, not too tight, but sexy, worn soft in the right places, and less splattered with proof of cooking than his black T-shirt.

As he bent to pull another pan from the refrigerator, I admired the roundness of his buns. He straightened and I averted my eyes to the pan extended from his Popeye forearms. In it two fish beseeched with dead eyes.

"I'm preparing the trout Szechwan style. I marinated these overnight in raspberry wine vinegar, fresh thyme and ground black pepper."

In sympathy my eyes bulged back at the fishes'.

"Oh, darling," he said, pronouncing it dahlin', "do the heads bother you? I'll remove them after I've baked the fish, even though the Chinese consider the eyeballs a delicacy." He slid the pan into the oven. "Everything's all set."

He clearly did not plan to tidy the kitchen. As for the living room, it was nearly empty except for a bulky armchair flanked by an upright crate full of books topped with a reading lamp. In the center of the room was a small table draped with lace table-cloth, and set with two white china plates, rose cloth napkins, two rose tapers in crystal holders, and a pink rose in a bud vase.

"Very elegant," I said as he seated me at the table, the only place we could sit together.

"Actually I owe it all to Punky."

"Punky?" Momentary panic clutched me. I could visualize them as a couple. They matched one another in emotional volatility.

"You know. Your neighbor? Our neighbor." He struck a match and lit the candles. "I went to borrow a candle to make the atmosphere a little more romantic, but when she wheedled out of me that I was going to use paper plates, she loaned me all this stuff." He shut off the lamp and sat across from me.

"Punky knows we have a . . . ." I searched for the right word. Could one call this a date?

"Are you embarrassed?" He sounded hurt. Candlelight soft-ened his face. It wasn't handsome, not in the G.Q. or even in the Sears Catalog fashion. It was rugged, even haggard, like a blond version of Charles Bronson, a face with character.

"The whole neighborhood will know."

"Are you embarrassed?" he repeated.

"No. But I'm a private person."

"Well, Miss Private Person, while I continue to torture those two little fishies in a three-hundred-seventy-five degree oven, would you like to look at my etchings?"

The End

"I can't believe he used that line," Lorraine chuckled.

I raked her with a scathing look, one that shut up or withered most disruptive students, even though she was my hostess, and I sat on her living room floor.

"And then what happened?" she pumped, undeterred.

"This isn't fair." I sipped my mug of coffee. "You want every detail, but you haven't even introduced me to your boyfriend."

"If you didn't go to bed with the chickens, you could have met Chuck a number of times." She maneuvered her wheelchair so it was closer to the side of her desk and her coffee. Or maybe she was just maneuvering away from the topic of her private life. "What time do you go to bed—eight thirty?"

"Nine," I corrected. The dark French roast Lorraine served was both richer and mellower than my cheap Bustello brand.

"Anyway, Malcolm asked if you wanted to see his etchings," she savored this information, "and . . . ?"

"And he showed me etchings."

"Seriously?"

"Lorraine, let me confide in you."

She leaned closer and looked about to tumble from her chair.

"I am the world's worst liar."

"That's all then?" she said.

"Well, he showed me his watercolors, too. He actually had

more watercolors than etchings."

"I don't believe it."

"Why?" I asked impatiently. "Is he usually a sex fiend?"

"No, but it does sound like you had a taming influence on him."

Great. Just what I wanted—a *taming influence* on men.

"Since you're firing all these personal questions at me, what about you and Chuck?" I said. "What's the nature of your relationship? Are you guys headed toward the altar?"

"I don't think so." She sighed. "Two old handicapped Vietnam Vets. We share memories and common problems. We're great friends, but we'd make lousy life-long mates."

"Why?"

"Too much in common."

"I've heard of too little in common." I thought of my last relationship. I had been wrong for Angelo. Not Greek. We'd grown up in different lands with different customs, different languages, and different religions. Angelo was a self-made man with less than a high school education while I'd spent seven years in college.

My pregnancy had forced us to see how unsuited we were for each other.

"Imagine two English teachers married," Lorraine said to clinch her point.

"God forbid." I crunched one of the chocolate-covered biscotti she'd offered with this mid-afternoon break. I had only a three-day workweek ahead and felt relatively relaxed, even sitting on the hard wood floor. "A nightmare." I pictured two English teachers propped in bed, both reading papers. Angelo, for all his faults, kissed and cuddled and curled around my back.

"Now take someone like Malcolm," Lorraine said.

I scooted more firmly against the wall. "Yes, let's take him."

"With that *joie de vivre*, he's a gem, but definitely in the rough. A lot of that bonhomie is nervous energy. It's like he must keep the patter going, or there might be silence. Or, worse yet, probing talk. He needs a calming influence, someone to polish him a bit."

I gathered she meant me. "The cat's enough," I said. "I have something important to do before I get involved. With anyone."

She fiddled with her cut-off pink sweat pants, tucking the ends neatly under her stumps. "What's that?"

"Writing."

"Are you a writer?" Her head bobbed up with rekindled interest.

"I don't deserve the title. I haven't written a word in almost two years."

Lorraine's eyes sharpened in attentiveness.

"A professor once advised me, 'Don't become a writer unless you have to.' Well, I had to. Even as a kid, I'd write these survival stories. My protagonists would get lost in the woods or some such and have to start making everything from scratch."

"Making a new life here should be a piece of cake then." She grinned.

I chewed my lip and reflected on my long-ago heroines. Even as a ten-year-old it seemed I'd been prepping myself to escape my hometown. Of course, in my stories, axes magically appeared so my character could hew trees to create a shelter. And my character knew how to do all of those things—build houses and make fires. Build a life out of nothing.

"When I was in high school," I continued, "I took a correspondence course in writing from U.C. Berkeley. That's kinda how I ended up out here."

"So what are you getting at?" Lorraine chomped on her biscotti. "What does all of this have to do with Mac?"

"I stopped writing so I could earn a living." My words caused a small sob, the quick intake of air sucking a bit of biscotti with it. My eyes teared.

Lorraine watched as I coughed and thumped my chest.

When I recovered, I said, "I woke up this morning and my fingers were tingling. All I could think about is this story in my head."

"What's the story?" she asked.

"Suffice it to say it's based on what's been happening here."

"Oh?" She raised an eyebrow.

"Fictionalized, of course."

"Of course." She waited a beat. "Am I in it?"

"Mmmmm. But you won't recognize yourself. I've changed your name to Gertrude."

"Gertrude!"

"Don't malign it. It's my mother's name."

Her face fell and she looked at the floor.

"I'm kidding." It felt good to rib her for a change, to feel my sense of humor reviving. "However, I'm changing your handicap."

Lorraine digested all of this. "Does this mean Malcolm's dust?"

I shrugged. "I don't need a man in my life, but I sure want one." I stood and stretched, empty mug in hand. "But I'm a first-year teacher, and I want to write. There won't be enough of me left for a relationship." I set the coffee cups and platter on her low kitchen counter. "Thanks a lot, Lorraine, but I have to get to work—lessons to plan and novels to write." And a cat to feed. And to name. Maybe *Milagro*. Miracle.

"I want to know the plot," Lorraine said.

"Hemingway said it's bad luck to talk about a story too much. A writer has to conserve that energy for the writing. But, here's the elevator pitch: an emotionally wounded young woman finds herself alone in an apartment complex that's so full of drama she can hardly process her own problems, but that turns out to be a good thing—a healing thing."

Needs work, I thought, leaning over her desk and peering out her window at my stoop. I squatted down and viewed how Lorraine would have seen me, lugging my book bag and purse into my apartment. At an angle, hulked the charred remains of Mrs. Bean's and with a twist, the laundry room and Florence's old place. It was a different perspective on our little neighborhood, but still much the same. In three months, the community had fluxed in and out, like a breathing organism, and I'd become part of it.

I turned to my friend. "When the protagonist gets to know everyone, she no longer feels cut off from the world. And, she has a story to write."

"I look forward to reading it," Lorraine said.

I floated across her room, engrossed in the world I would create. Who would enter through those magical fictional doors? *Mac?*

"Good luck," Lorraine called, but her words barely registered.

When I settled before my typewriter, Milagro instantly jumped into my lap. I stroked her multi-colored ruff, thinking of the poem *Pied Beauty*—*Glory be to God for dappled things.* The sonnet praised the *counter, original, spare and strange.* All part of creation.

Milagro snuggled in and purred. I started the novel with the setting, a sense of place. I was usually weak on this. I never enjoyed reading descriptive passages, so I tended not to write them. This time I'd make sure my reader had a sense of place— these ugly, mustard-colored apartments on Lostart Street.

ACKNOWLEDGMENTS

Lostart Street has passed through two writing groups. Along the way, the book has gathered new bits. Sentences have been spit polished. Darlings have been cut. I owe many thanks to the writing groups members. The first group included: Anna Citrino, Sharlya Gold, Erica Lann-Clark, and Bob O'Brien. Members of the second writing group included: Jack Jones, Rick Parfitt, Cheri Wells, Chris Goddard, Lynda Scott, Chris Beal and Sandy Losik. Thank you all! I am also grateful for my beta readers Patricia Denke, Cindy Klassen, Margie Bunting, and Lynda Scott. All we have is time, and they generously gave me some of theirs. Crystal Edwards also offered an abundance of love through her work on my author photo.

Finally, as with all my books thus far, *Lostart Street* wouldn't exist without the wonderful women at misterio press.

ABOUT THE AUTHOR

Vinnie Hansen fled the howling winds of the South Dakota prairie and headed for the California coast the day after high school graduation.

As a child, she read books while huddled on top the dryer. Vinnie grew up to write numerous short stories and the Carol Sabala mystery series. The seventh installment in the series, BLACK BEANS & VENOM, made the finalist list for the Claymore Award.

Still sane after 27 years of teaching high school English, Vinnie has retired and lives in Santa Cruz, California, with her husband and the requisite cat.

Please visit her website at http://vinniehansen.com or find her on Facebook or Goodreads. Authors live and die by reviews. If you enjoyed Lostart Street, post something.

vinniehansen.com